Lost and Found

THE CHESHIRE PRIZE FOR LITERATURE ANTHOLOGIES

Prize Flights: Stories from the Cheshire Prize for Literature 2003; edited by Ashley Chantler

Life Lines: Poems from the Cheshire Prize for Literature 2004; edited by Ashley Chantler

Word Weaving: Stories and Poems for Children from the Cheshire Prize for Literature 2005; edited by Jaki Brien

Edge Words: Stories from the Cheshire Prize for Literature 2006; edited by Peter Blair

Elements: Poems from the Cheshire Prize for Literature 2007; edited by Peter Blair

Wordscapes: Stories and Poems for Children from the Cheshire Prize for Literature 2008; edited by Jaki Brien

Zoo: Short Stories from the Cheshire Prize for Literature 2009; edited by Emma L. E. Rees

Still Life: Poetry from the Cheshire Prize for Literature 2010; edited by Emma L. E. Rees

Wordlife: Stories and Poems for Children from the Cheshire Prize for Literature 2011; edited by Jaki Brien

Lost and Found

Short Stories from the Cheshire Prize for Literature 2012

Edited by Emma L. E. Rees

University of Chester Press

First Published 2013
by University of Chester Press
Parkgate Road
Chester CH1 4BJ

Printed and bound in the UK by the
LIS Print Unit
University of Chester
Cover designed by the LIS Graphics Team
University of Chester

Editorial Material
© University of Chester, 2013
Foreword and Stories
© the respective authors, 2013

All Rights Reserved
No part of this publication may be reproduced, stored in a retrieval system or transmitted in any form or by any means without the prior permission of the copyright owner, other than as permitted by UK copyright legislation or under the terms and conditions of a recognised copyright licensing scheme

A catalogue record of this book is available from the British Library

ISBN 978-1-908258-10-6

Nicky Claire Troke
18.09.74 – 07.03.13

CONTENTS

Contributors	x
Foreword	xxii
Udumbara in Lytham St Anne's *Sarah Frost Mellor*	1
The Gift *Adam Green*	8
Taidi's Big Party *Simon Gotts*	14
The Adventures of Him and Her *Hannah Riordan*	20
The Inheritance *Sophie Green*	27
17 Hours Across State *Barbara Corfield*	34
Part of the Furniture *Richard Lakin*	40
The Library *Sarah Leigh*	47

Lost and Found

Small Accommodations *Angi Holden*	53
Window Dressing *Lynne Parry-Griffiths*	59
A View to a Kill *Don Nixon*	65
Postcard from Delanos, Wichita *Lynne Voyce*	71
Dangerous Tuesday *Angela Williams*	77
The Shadow *Laura Harrhy*	84
Mr Mystery's Lion *Clare Kirwan*	90
Watching *Valerie West*	96
Emeralds *Anne-Marie Biggs*	102
Panada *Tanya D. Ravenswater*	111

Contents

Scut, or, the Rabbit's Tale   118
Mike Wood

Butcher's Grass   123
Die Booth

Blood Flies Upwards   129
Elizabeth Brassington

A Search for Simeon   134
George Horsman

Tighten the Cord Around his Neck   141
Andrew Bogle

The Killer Sentence   147
Miriam Sulhunt

CONTRIBUTORS

Anne-Marie Biggs spent many happy years in Cheshire in Lymm and Bowdon as a child, then in Stockport while young, free and single, and later lived with her own family near Macclesfield. She has two smallish children who never understand that Mummy really would like more time to write, and she works as a university administrator for projects based in Africa, despite not being all that keen on travel! She enjoys gardening and walking and is currently terracing her garden, which seemed like a good idea at the time. She relocated to Warwickshire recently and is getting used to life in the Midlands.

Andrew Bogle lives with his family in Appleton. He spent his teenage years in Wilmslow where the ancient Lindow Man, also dubbed "Lindow Pete", was unearthed in a peat bog. Andrew's short story "Tighten the Cord Around His Neck", was inspired by the corpse's grisly end. His previous publications include "Debt Recovery in Europe". Inexplicably no one has yet snapped up the rights to a Hollywood musical version. Until then, or if a publisher is found for his glittering novel set on Italy's Amalfi coast, Andrew continues with the day job as a solicitor in Chester with Walker Smith Way.

Die Booth lives in Chester in a tiny house with four fireplaces and enjoys playing violin, drinking tea and

exploring dark places. Die's work has featured in two previous Cheshire Prize anthologies and has most recently appeared in *The Fiction Desk*, *Litro*, *For All Eternity* from Dark Opus Press and Prime's *Bloody Fabulous* anthology, among others. You can also read several of Die's stories in the 2011 anthology *Re-Vamp*, co-edited by Die and L. C. Hu. Forthcoming work is due to appear in *The Art of Fairytales*, edited by Sarah Grant, and Die's first novel, *Spirit Houses*, a tale of possession, betrayal, action, adventure and excellent Scotch, will be available in 2013.
Website: http://diebooth.wordpress.com/

Elizabeth Brassington qualified many, many years ago as a teacher in Cheshire, and this has always remained her favourite county. In the 1970s she wrote scripts for *Mandy*, a girls' comic, which was great fun, and her writing has also appeared in other magazines, including *Yours*, *Best*, *Tears in the Fence* and *Mslexia*. She has had children's stories on BBC national and local radio and, over the years, has won various competitions. In 2007, her "Henry" topped *The Sun* newspaper's short story competition and was adapted for inclusion in *The Sun Book of Short Stories*, part of an Adult Literacy series. Most recently she has had poems published in *The Oldie* – a suitable market for someone of her advanced years! – and she continues to dive in head first whenever a writing opportunity presents itself.

Barbara Corfield's life is not always commensurate with that of the stereotyped brooding and isolated writer. Married with two young children, her story writing is often interrupted by a direct hit from a paper aeroplane or distractive arguments over the television remote control ownership. However, from the chaos, Barbara draws upon the fragility of childhood emotions, family bonds and real-life events to create enduring and relatable characters. With a background in the Humanities, and qualifications in Counselling, Barbara embarked on writing relatively recently following the completion of an inspiring Creative Writing course. The inclusion of her story "17 Hours Across State" in this Anthology will be her first publication, and this, so early on in her writing career, gives her great encouragement to continue doing what she loves.

Sarah Frost Mellor lives in Bristol with her husband and daughter, where she writes quirky copy for a well-loved travel publisher. She's also worked as a bookseller, and with the Royal Navy. An award-winning short-story writer, Sarah's debut novel, *Someone Else's Skin*, will be published by Headline in February 2014 under her pen name, Sarah Hilary. It will be followed a year later by a second novel, *Long Gone*. Sarah has never owned a Typhoon Crusader, but has often enjoyed reading the names of caravans as she passes them on the motorway. She hopes never to aspire to a chemical lavatory.

Contributors

Website: www.sarah-crawl-space.blogspot.co.uk/
Twitter: @Sarah_Hilary

Simon Gotts works as a librarian in North Wales, where most of his stories are now set. He lived in Chester for many years and benefited greatly during that time by being a member of Chester Writers. His stories and poems have featured in a number of Cheshire Prize anthologies.

Adam Green, originally from Manchester, spent several years in Berlin and now lives in London. When not reading and writing he spends his time drowning in various parts of the internet as editor of *The Public Domain Review*, an online journal dedicated to curating and showcasing the most interesting out-of-copyright works on the web.

Sophie Green writes short stories, children's fiction, comedy and plays. Her novel *The Last Giant* was shortlisted for the Times/Chicken House Children's Fiction Competition 2011. Her short stories have been published in *Lip;* an anthology for IP1 magazine, on Ether Books and in the Bridport Winners' Anthology 2012. She lived in Eastham on the Wirral in the nineties while studying for a degree in Zoology at Liverpool University. She now lives in Suffolk and works in two public libraries. If she didn't spend all her spare time reading and writing she would have enjoyed cooking, gardening and going to the cinema.

Lost and Found

Website: www.thelastgiant.com
Twitter: @greensofe

Laura Harrhy found that, after living in London, Paris, Heidelberg, Granada and Madrid (though not all at the same time), a simple walk along the banks of the River Dee one summer's day was inspiration enough for her to make Cheshire her home, and it is a joyful place to read, write and live. As is usual for writers, she has written and read for as long as she has been able; that is, since the day she was fitted with glasses. She splits her spare time between daydreaming up new stories and scenarios, and shooing pigeons off her balcony. Then, when she's run out of ways to procrastinate, she practises her clarinet, and when the weather is warm, she rows on the Dee, or (tries to) rock climb with her other half.

Angi Holden has, tucked away in a cupboard, a partially-made patchwork quilt, which is pretty much symbolic of her writing life. She gathers a plethora of scraps of various colours and textures – overheard conversations, family tales, photographs and sketches, news stories, maps, memories. She stitches them together. Sometimes the patterns that emerge are intentional; more often they are accidental. The surprise is always the juxtaposition of one element against another, whether the outcome is a poem, a short story or a flash-fiction. Just as she doubts she will ever complete her quilt, she hopes she will never stop writing.

George Horsman found Chester a pleasantly sleepy city as a schoolboy there and so has returned after retiring from academic life. He has had many poems and stories published or broadcast, some of which have won awards. He finds that choral singing, playing clarinet and tennis, hillwalking and doing crosswords, help to keep him awake.

Clare Kirwan lives in Wirral. Like the girl in the story, she used to be a magician's assistant, but rarely jumps out of empty boxes any more. She has had poems and stories published widely including in *Mslexia*, *The North*, and has won various prizes in poetry and short fiction contests. Her new (unpublished) novel – *The Undead Residents' Association* – was a finalist in Pulp Idol 2012. By day she is a library assistant, like Batgirl.
Website: www.clarekirwan.co.uk
Twitter: @ClareKirwan

Richard Lakin has worked as a labourer, chemist, policeman, salesman and journalist, among other jobs. After years of writing while commuting he needs loud mobile phone conversations, random platform announcements and luggage in the way before he can pen a word. He is a member of Writing West Midlands Room 204 writers' development programme. His work has been published by *The*

Lost and Found

Guardian, Daily Telegraph, Cheshire Prize for Literature, *Notes from the Underground,* Oxford University's *Oxonian Review,* the University of Dundee and other anthologies. He lives in Staffordshire with his wife, two sons and an indomitable Jack Russell.
Website: richlakin.wordpress.com
Twitter: @Lakinwords

Sarah Leigh loves travelling. She's ridden a camel around the Thar Desert, visited floating reed islands in Lake Titicaca and walked along sand dunes in the Sahara. Her favourite place was camping above the clouds on the Inca Trail. She also loves skiing, curries and writing Clerihews. Following a childhood in Cheshire, Sarah studied philosophy at Leeds University and went on to London to work in publishing and then as a literary agent. She is now a full-time mum of two boys, but managed to squeeze in an MA in Creative Writing from Manchester University in 2011. She lives in Knutsford, Cheshire, and is currently working on a novel and a children's book. *London Magazine* once published one of her stories and she won the Write Northwest competition in 2012 with "Dare", due out in an anthology from Erbacce Press in 2013.

Don Nixon has published a number of short stories (mainly in the crime genre) in this country and North America. Wearing his other hat, he writes poetry and has won various competitions including the formal award at the Italian Poetry On The Lake Festival in 2010 and 2011 and the Leeds Peace Poetry Festival in 2012. His first novel, *Ransom*, in the Western adventure genre was published in January 2013. In November 2012 he had two crime short stories published in the Crime Anthology *Crime After Crime*. Both of these books are available in print and on download from Amazon. He had a short story published in the 2006 Cheshire Prize for Literature anthology *Edge Words* (2006), and this encouraged him to start to write.

Lynne Parry-Griffiths was born in North Wales in a former workhouse and educated in an adjoining building and at various universities. She read English Literature before attending the same drama school, though not at the same time, as Dame Helen Mirren and Alan Carr. Since then she has taught and examined both English Literature and Language and is currently a part-time A-Level tutor. A self-confessed history geek, her obsessions include the Salem Witch Trials, English Baroque portraitist William Dobson, and the First World War. Welsh-speaking, fond of rugby union and loud music, she has two cats, is a vegetarian and claims to be perfectly normal.

Tanya D. Ravenswater is originally from Co. Down, Northern Ireland, from a home where stories, poetry and humour are considered almost as essential for good health as daily peas, eggs and potatoes. She is sincerely grateful to her parents for encouraging her to prefer life in eccentric, light and dark fairy-tale worlds, where all manner of beasts and people have a place. When not pretending to be Rapunzel and looking after her own ogre, teenage elves and friendly wolf, Tanya writes for adults and children. She particularly enjoys spending time with young word wizards in primary schools inviting them to discover their own forms of magic and spelling.

Emma L. E. Rees was chair of the judges of the 2012 Cheshire Prize for Literature, and is the editor of this anthology. She's a senior lecturer in the Department of English, where she's worked since moving to the University of Chester from UEA in 1999. Her most recent book is *The Vagina: A Literary and Cultural History* (Bloomsbury, 2013), a fact which makes her mother proud and embarrassed in pretty equal measure.

Hannah Riordan declared at the age of five that she had no interest in writing anything given that she could already read. She later revised that opinion and spent the vast majority of her teenage years scribbling into notebooks with the hope of making it work as a career, much to the dismay of her teachers. However, she was eventually accepted into the University of Chester to study Creative Writing with English Literature and now spends her time reading, working on her novels, daydreaming and attending ballet classes. She sometimes thinks she might have let her five-year-old self down slightly.

Miriam Sulhunt churns out poetry and short stories behind net curtains in douce Morningside, occasionally venturing out for walks with her greyhound, then home to pen more wistful tales for the women's weeklies. She has had modest success with her poetry, some of which has appeared in magazines and anthologies. Mostly, she writes light verse and, as with her fiction, draws on her own life for ideas. For some years, she tutored visiting Italian Air Force pilots and this experience often made her and her students laugh out loud, though one did text a friend that he wished he were dead. On which note, perhaps she should add that any resemblance to persons living or dead in this particular story, "The Killer Sentence", is purely coincidental (especially all you members of the Edinburgh Writers' Club).

Lynne Voyce lives in Birmingham with her husband and two daughters, where she teaches English at an inner city comprehensive school. Her short fiction has been published widely and she has won many competitions, including: Momaya, Legend, Calderdale Short Story Award and Flash 500. She is awaiting the publication of her first short story collection by an independent press and is currently working on her first novel. She would like to be fluent in French, cook fantastic vegetarian food and complete Wainwright's

Coast to Coast Walk, but right now she doesn't have the time.

Valerie West guesses that she fits into the stereotype of retired spinster, though she is between cats at the moment. She has lived in England, Scotland and Wales and settled in Cheshire twenty years ago. Her working life was divided between librarianship and the professional theatre, where she worked as a stage manager and in administration, helping to put on plays in a wide variety of venues from the West End to village halls. Her final post was as a School Librarian which was hard work, sometimes stressful, often entertaining and she learned a lot. She hopes that the boys picked up something along the way too. Now retired, her time is spent on idling, voluntary work and a long-delayed inclination to write.

Angela Williams was born and raised in Sydney, but left the other side of the world for love of a good Englishman and, after much travel to exotic places, they are now settled in Cheshire with their son. A former historic buildings conservation officer and DJ, her greatest pleasures in life are writing, and shoes. She was instrumental in the flowering of the Ashton Hayes Writers Group, and is currently writing a novel while studying for an MA in Creative Writing. This is her first short story, and it is also the first that she has had published which, in her words, is "even better than winning the lottery the first time you buy a ticket".

Mike Wood is a poet but occasionally is persuaded to write short stories. He has a playful love of words inspired by a wide life experience as a headteacher, manager of a homeless charity and of a young people's hostel in Snowdonia. He once taught a class on April Fool's Day that time was going to be decimalised and that an hour would be subdivided into 100 deci-hours. Married to Andrea, he now has four grandchildren, two of whom live in West Africa, and he is a qualified counsellor.

FOREWORD

In the autumn of 2007, a Cheshire charity shop was the rather unlikely setting for an incident which proved that life does, in fact, often imitate art. An old handbag donated to the Nantwich branch of Oxfam was found to contain a rare first edition of Oscar Wilde's *The Importance of Being Earnest*. The owner of the handbag could not be traced, so the book was sold by the shop for £650. Anyone familiar with Wilde's play will recognise at once the eerie resonances of this story. In *Earnest*, John ("Jack") Worthing, when he's not busy being Ernest in the city, is hopelessly in love with Gwendolen Fairfax. Gwendolen's general air of vacuity and Jack's secret identity are but two obstacles in the lovers' apparently ill-fated courtship. It's a relationship which is overseen by Gwendolen's imperious mother, Lady Bracknell, who rebels when she discovers Jack's unpropitious origins. In Anthony Asquith's iconic 1952 film production of the play, Michael Redgrave stars as Jack, opposite Edith Evans's pitilessly doughty Lady Bracknell. "I said I had lost my parents," declares Jack, continuing: "It would perhaps be nearer the truth to say that my parents seem to have lost me". Jack was, as fans of the play will know, "found" by a "charitable gentleman" in "a handbag" (and if you can't *hear* Edith Evans's immortal, extruded delivery of those two potent words, do find Asquith's film on YouTube).

Foreword

The Nantwich handbag owner's loss was, of course, very much Oxfam's gain. In deciding to call this anthology *Lost and Found*, I'm thinking of how much of simply being human involves an almost indiscernible daily bookkeeping – an accounting for both small and, sometimes, monumental, losses and gains. So what is "lost" and "found" in the stories in this collection? Losing oneself in the foggy agonies of Alzheimer's is the theme of one story; others focus on loss and grief, or on the potency of material mementoes. Children lose their childhoods, and adults find happiness and emptiness in almost equal measure. Words are found in order to express loss. Serendipity is a guiding force in many of the stories: repeatedly, chance encounters resulting in loss or discovery, are vividly evoked.

There were more than 260 entrants to the 2012 Cheshire Prize short story competition in total (twenty-four of those have made it through to publication in this anthology). Those 260 original entries exhibited an extraordinary breadth of subject matter, ranging in their settings from the Far East to suburbia; from the Iron Age to a dystopian future; and from the Antipodes to the snowy wastes. Rather oddly, murder was a key theme: many stories entered for the competition (and some included in this anthology, too) were concerned with doing away with people in unwholesome, but frequently delightfully inventive, ways. Relationships featured prominently, too: between parents and children; between lovers;

between partners in – frequently – *loveless* relationships, and there were also some really thought-provoking explorations of the individual's relationship to him or herself. Happily (as I remarked at the awards evening), there were significantly fewer stories submitted to the 2012 competition about werewolves and vampires than there have been in recent years. This is definitely a trend to be both celebrated and encouraged.

The twenty-four writers have displayed patience and efficiency throughout the various editorial stages, and for that I thank them most warmly. Each story in this anthology is, by definition, worthy of publication, but the judges felt that four contributions were exceptionally good. The overall winner of the 2012 Prize was Sarah Frost Mellor for her powerful story "Udumbara in Lytham St Anne's". Here, the mundane is quite brilliantly and skilfully juxtaposed with the almost-magical. Perhaps more than any other story in the collection, Sarah's suggested the idea of "lost and found" to me, since it strongly shows the transformative powers of an imagination which can find beauty in the most unlikely places. Adam Green won second prize for his uncanny story, "The Gift", and Simon Gotts ("Taidi's Big Party") and Hannah Riordan ("The Adventures of Him and Her") were both highly commended.

I would also like to thank those many colleagues who helped with the judging process. I'm particularly grateful to my co-judges, Francesca Haig and John

Foreword

Scrivener, and the input of these colleagues early on in the selection process was invaluable: Derek Alsop, Peter Blair, Matt Davies, Melissa Fegan, Sarah Heaton, Frank Herrmann, Clara Neary, Yvonne Siddle, William Stephenson, Sally West, Richard E. Wilson. I'm very grateful to Loyd Grossman OBE, FSA, for reading out the winning entry at the awards evening in December 2012, and to the High Sheriff of Cheshire, William Lees-Jones, for announcing the winners' names and presenting them with their prizes. I've also received much help from, and exchanged countless emails with, the University of Chester's Corporate Communications team, in particular Jayne Dodgson and Jenni Westcott. Sarah Griffiths continues to be a wonderfully resourceful general editor for the University of Chester Press. Sponsorship by Bank of America Europe Card Services has allowed the competition to flourish and I am very grateful for their continuing support.

Finally, I dedicate this anthology to the memory of my husband's cousin, Nicky Troke, whose wedding we went to in the New Forest in September 2012, only to return for her funeral in March 2013. Even when Nicky knew that she was dying, she did not mourn her losses, but instead rejoiced in all that she had *found* in her too-short life.

Emma L. E. Rees
Chair, Judging Panel, and Editor, *Lost and Found*
Department of English, University of Chester
2 May 2013

UDUMBARA IN LYTHAM ST ANNE'S

Sarah Frost Mellor

Towards the end of our time together, my mother communicated in cutlery. A semaphore of place settings, three of everything, waiting for a remark from me to remind her it was just the two of us now.

After lunch, she'd unravel another of Dad's jumpers, because she couldn't bear anything to go to waste. No words would be spoken. She'd bring her knitting basket and I'd kneel with my hands up, spooling the wool as she pulled it loose, winding it into a skein to join the rest of the undone knitwear.

Everything was back to front, just then; soon, she'd start planning her funeral. She was talking about putting in a downstairs toilet, "For when I can't manage the stairs any longer." An estate agent, with belligerent optimism, had suggested the pantry could be made over as a lavatory.

"Your father favours a chemical," she told me, taking a tin of custard powder from the pantry shelf. "But I could never stoop to that."

I liked to read the papers in the afternoon, when it was quiet in the house. On Lushan Mountain in China, I read, a nun had found a flower growing under her washing machine, so rare it blossomed only once every three thousand years.

Lost and Found

I studied the photograph of the Udumbara, its petals questing upwards in tentative, translucent tongues of white. I was surprised that nuns used washing machines, pictured them separating wimples from habits, although I knew this to be an oversimplified view of their apparel.

You probably need to be a nun to find an exquisitely rare flower blooming in your kitchen. Not much chance of such domestic paradise in Lytham St Anne's. But I looked, just in case, on the pretext of a spring clean. Under Mum's washing machine, I found twenty pence, a green wine gum and a fistful of fluff.

"Wine gums," she said heavily. "Your father's favourite."

We lived in a redbrick house by the seaside, although you couldn't see the sea from any of its windows. When I was small, my parents would walk me once a month down to the front, to look at the flat tarnish of the Irish Sea.

Hard to imagine a less eventful coastline. No cresting waves or rearing sky. No gulls sweeping in to sabotage the beach's blandly freckled face. Just the skin of the water pulled up tight as a bedcover, from the horizon to the shingle edge.

They'd stand me there for ten minutes, eyeing the horizon's flatline as if to say, "Just as we thought, nothing to see here."

I'd sometimes pull away, jumping down the iron steps to poke about on the beach, pocketing a stone or two for appearance's sake.

When I came back up the steps, Dad would make me empty my pockets.

"It's against the law to take stones from the beach," he'd say in a tone that managed to convey both his antipathy towards the pettifogging tyranny of this law and his deep satisfaction with it.

I was the daughter of their middle age, a fact they told me plainly and often. I was much the way you might expect, having been raised by two people with little in their lives and no love lost between them. My appearance was placid, my outlook unambitious. Other parents might've thought me a disappointment. But mine liked disappointment; they knew where they stood with it.

Dad would sometimes say of me, "She's a good head on her shoulders," meaning that I expected nothing from life and that my realism was to be applauded.

I was not a rebellious teenager. Given the way things have worked out, however, I can't say that I'm sorry.

When Joe first came to the door, he was carrying a plastic crate which held half a dozen bottles of One-Chem Cassette Cleaner.

Mum refused to deal with him: "Tell him to drive round the back."

Joe didn't mind. He had to knock at the front door, he explained, it was company policy. He carried the crate to Dad's Crusader Typhoon, beached on bricks.

"Sorry about this," I said, meaning the inconvenience or maybe the daft name on the caravan's broad white rump.

"No problem," Joe smiled.

His name was on a badge pinned to his blue shirt. The back of his neck was pink from the sun. His nose was freckled, like his forearms.

He came often after that, in prompt response to Dad's frequent emails.

Inside, the Crusader Typhoon smelt of the chemical Dad favoured, a blue solution in which his stools skulked and grew fuzzy. The scent of the chemical slugged it out with a top note of industrial pine; he'd hung as bunting three dozen air fresheners purchased on special offer, pine trees in contrasting colours, green and orange and red. The effect was jolly I'd give him that, but the smell would make your eyes water.

It was always too hot in the Typhoon. Dad lived in shorts and T-shirts. Realising he'd no need of knitwear, Mum set about reclaiming the wool from his jumpers and pullovers. We never saw him in the house, and he rarely saw us. But he was there, at the foot of the garden, a happy crusader in his caravan.

Udumbara in Lytham St Anne's

It was Joe he wanted, the bringer of dried food and bin liners and the coveted free samples, batteries, lip seal and lubricant.

"Thanks," I'd say, each time there was a fresh delivery.

"No problem," Joe would smile.

Dad bought the caravan in the summer of '74. The summer of the St Anne's pier blaze.

"The open road!" Dad's eyes shone, and so did mine.

Then he got sidetracked by the business of waste management. The Crusader Typhoon sat in a dull stew of dust on the cinder path all summer.

Princess Anne came to Yehudi Menuhin's concert that July. The town was made up with itself, until the fire. They found the pier's fireproof safe buried in the mud next morning, after the lounge floor fell in. Experts blew the safe open. That was a pretty exciting summer.

Not that Dad noticed. He talked of nothing but waste carriers and bowl cleaner, bringing home samples of toilet tissue for us to test. He wanted to see which brand fulfilled the promise of "Soft use and rapid dissolve", quizzing salesmen on the chemistry involved. "What's the percentage of formaldehyde?" "What dosage do you recommend for a family of three with an above average fibre intake?"

Dad was obsessed with fibre. He'd sprinkle it in supplement form onto bowls already filled with bran.

Lost and Found

He was a great advocate of what he called, "A good ridding", which perhaps explained how he was happy to live in a caravan while Mum, a terrific hoarder, liked the house to herself.

If you were to ask which came first, my father's high fibre diet or his fascination with waste management, I couldn't say. I only know that the summer I was seven, the summer Princess Anne and Yehudi Menuhin came to Lytham, the Crusader Typhoon didn't shift from its spot at the bottom of the garden. Dad spent hours getting it ready for when we'd hit the open road.

We haven't hit it yet, I'm pleased to say.

It was Joe introduced Dad to formaldehyde-free chemical cleaner. You can't whack it, Dad says. I've never seen him so happy.

As for Mum, Joe's put up shelves in the kitchen for her recipe books. On Sundays, she lays three places at the table, and Joe and I eat with her. Mum's knitting Joe a jumper, to say thanks for the shelves.

I ride with Joe in his van nearly every day, so I'm never far from the caravan or the house. We share his bedsit over the fish and chip shop on the front. Our bathroom's behind a beaded curtain, under a skylight.

Sometimes we go down to the beach and lie in the empty pockets of shingle, looking out to Ireland and imagining all the places we'll explore. Bouvet Island. Tristan da Cunha. But mostly we stay in the bedsit.

Udumbara in Lytham St Anne's

I love to watch Joe take a shower, the way the water runs over the peaks of his shoulders, and around the hollows of his hips.

He is my miracle. Found by accident, in the least likely of places. A little bit of Lushan Mountain come to Lytham St Anne's.

I sit on the bed and count the rosary of the beaded curtain as he washes off the day.

Through the skylight, the sun falls on him and his skin shines until it's singing.

I think, "There's still so much of him I haven't seen," but I'm in no hurry, being lazy by nature and having inherited something of my parents' satisfaction with the status quo.

THE GIFT

Adam Green

Rising up to the crest of dunes, through the tall thin grass and out onto the brow, Stephen and Sophie came in sight of the beach. They could not at first make sense of what they saw. There appeared to be hundreds and hundreds of bodies, naked, pale, sunbathing in all manner of strange contortions. Then they saw, by the plastic sheen in the sunlight, that they were not people but mannequin dolls. Apart from the occasional wooden crate almost all of it seemed to be mannequins, many broken apart, spanning the whole shore from end to rocky end in a great curve of pink and dislocated parts. Beyond the debris line they could see the sea bring in more, long waves crashing in heavy with bodies, the foamy drift of a leg or a twisting head, the rotating spins of chests and breasts. They watched in silence, taking in the bizarreness of the scene, and then, hand in hand, they descended to the beach. As they made their way into the spread of figures, they parted hands to take a closer look. Stephen knelt down before one near intact, missing only an arm – a woman, bleached pale, eyes and slight smile face down to the sand. Across her smooth solid back lay a piece of seaweed glistening now in the sunlight. All around it, across the curves of her body, the blades of her shoulders, the nape of her neck, the rise of buttocks and crevice of knees, there had already formed a thin crust of salt. At her feet he saw a tiny pool had formed in the hollow between the ankle bone and the Achilles heel. He shuffled over and dipped a finger in. It was warm, a small ring of salt at its waterline. He stood up again, his wet finger to the breeze, observing the chaos of figures – arms akimbo, legs splayed, hips thrust in posing. There was something strange in how they all gazed off course, obliviously so, at unplanned angles, not on the horizontal for which their poses were fashioned, but off instead into sand or to sky. He stood there awhile lost in their angles, constellations of arrangement, taken over by a peculiar kind of calm. About halfway down the beach, rising up from the figures, he could see Sophie standing, looking out to sea with an arm in her hands.

"Have you seen how worn they are? They must have come for miles, for months."

Sophie didn't answer. She watched the waves crashing in, the occasional figure or limb being laid to rest, shifting a little with the tidal retreat. Further out she could see that even more were coming, the water dense with the floating debris.

Stephen made his way over to where she was stood. "I said they must have come for miles."

She didn't turn. He could see that she was lost in serious thought – that wrinkling of her brow, little tighten of the mouth. She went to speak, but stopped and looked down confused at the arm in her hand. She turned to face him.

"Why is it here? It's so weird. There's so many of them."

He looked out to sea to where they continued to arrive. "It must be from a ship. Spilled cargo from a storm. And I guess the current just took it this way."

She seemed in some way unsatisfied by his answer. She turned back to the ocean. "I mean, why today? It's so strange it should be today."

"What do you mean?"

"That it's today. For our anniversary."

Stephen felt something suddenly plummet between them. As she turned to face him again he could see that slight manic shade in her gaze, a strange train of thought flitting behind her eyes. These mannequins had come, as if summoned to join her clouding mood, to force it now to some kind of climax. He was struck suddenly by how blue her eyes looked, how they matched her socks, two bands round the ankles above her snow-white shoes. As he looked at her there, the bodies at her feet, he imagined her suddenly not on the beach but standing in a field, the day after a battle, as in that painting he'd seen, the mannequins, the spread of death-strewn bodies, the horses, mud, all caught in that slant of morning light. And her just standing there among it all. Maybe a mother, sister or lover, looking for someone. Maybe still alive. And as he looked at her now it seemed she was doing just this, scanning the scene for some sign of life. Then she suddenly straightened, seeming to see it, eyes hardening to a point.

The Gift

"Let's see what's in the boxes over there."

He followed her gaze over to the few wooden crates which lay gathered by the rocks at the far end of the beach. They were huge, chest-height. With a new urgency she led the way to the nearest, circling its sides with her quick little steps, running her hand along the fractured seam. Stephen felt a tug of panic. He could feel her going, lost now to some other narrative, her every gesture gathered towards a point which seemed to lie beyond the simple presence of these washed-up dolls. To some kind of image, an increasingly determined hope. As he watched her pick up a stone from her feet and begin to bash the open edge, he saw now this image to which she seemed to be drawn. A hope that in the box there'd be something different, the stuff of life, stories – art, letters, diaries, a photograph album – anything to which she could attach a meaning, to make sense of the ridiculous scene around them, to clothe this weird spread of anonymous plastic. To make sense of whatever horrifying message she had seen traced in the twisted arrangement of limbs, which perhaps was nonsense and so doubly terrifying. Stephen wondered why now it felt like a move away from him. He couldn't, and didn't want to, leave the beach, the sunlight, the breeze, the calm spread of these bodies. He didn't want anything else. He wanted to lie down with her among them. He looked back out to the surf laden with figures, the soundtrack of the waves and the rhythm of Sophie's stone upon the box.

And then he heard a crack.

He looked round to see her removing the lid. He went over and together they peered into the box. They gazed down upon one of those storage bags with the zips and handles, patterned with blue and red checks on white. Her hands trembling a little, Sophie undid the zip and as the sides fell away they saw the contents. A surface of dark and sodden denim. Stacks and stacks of blue jeans neatly folded. And then the smell hit them, the sharp rankness of rotting. Despite it, Sophie reached inside, as in a trance, stone-faced. She brought out a pair of the soaked wet jeans and let them unfurl from her chest to her feet.

"My God, they're huge," said Stephen.

They were indeed huge. At least double the width of a normal waist. Each leg massive, like the trunk of a tree. From the top of the waist Sophie looked so small, at each of the ends her little white hands holding tight. She didn't say anything. These were not her letters of love and life, these were jeans for fat people. Stephen went to the bag and pulled out another pair just the same. They rifled through the rest. They were all huge, slight variations in size, but all absolutely huge. They began to spread them out one by one on the surrounding rocks. The bag was now empty and they removed it to see an identical one beneath. Sophie paused for a moment, staring down at this second bag. Then she opened it and again saw the texture of sodden denim, this time not blue, but a wetted red. Once more, mechanically, she began to take the jeans out and lay them on the rocks. A little off to the side Stephen watched her at work, her tiny figure hauling the huge sodden gifts, her mouth tight with effort and her eyes, it seemed, now softened, glistening, perhaps even smiling at the hole opened up, and at how the breeze came in and, through it, sunlight, and how he joined her now and together they worked at the arranging of the jeans, taking great care, creating on the rocks a sprawling pattern of blues and reds.

TAIDI'S BIG PARTY

Simon Gotts

"I think he's too young." His Mum, behind the half-closed door.

"Eleven, these days, Lynn, they know everything. They've seen it all on TV ... video games." His favourite great aunty, always a good sign if she was in the kitchen.

"I know it seems like that, Meira, but he's quiet. He reads more than he watches TV."

If it was a party, why shouldn't he go? But then his Mum said *sensitive* and he knew what it was. It was Taidi. Taidi's big party. Aunty Meira was right. Of course he was going. They couldn't bloody stop him.

***

They rode around the streets in a black people carrier with tinted windows. Like the Mafia. He looked out at all the people in the sunlit town, staring as much as he wanted. They couldn't stare back or ask what he was lookin' at, pal? He shot them down for a while, then the car got caught in traffic. It heated up inside and the driver put on the air conditioning. Kyle felt the sweat dry cold on his chest and arms. He had nothing on under his stiff white shirt. His Mum had bought half a dozen for when he started High School, hoping they would still fit him in September if he stuck to his diet.

When the lads at school found out they thought it was cool. A funeral. You get to dress up, like *Men in Black*. Do you see it? The dead body? *That's my Taid. He's not a dead body. He's a person.* Yeah, a dead person. Someone made a choking noise and stuck their tongue out the side of their mouth. But they were right. It was cool. Paying his Respects.

"The Streets of Laredo." He couldn't get the song out of his head. He was learning it on Taidi's old guitar. It's no use to me now, Taidi had said. You never know, it might give you some street cred. And if that fails you can whack those bastard High School bullies in the kisser with it. Kyle hummed the song softly. Except he changed it in his head to "The Streets of Llandudno". He stopped for a moment at the word breast. Shot in the breast. He thought about breasts, looked around for them on the street, among the shoppers dawdling past the static traffic. But he had to admit he wasn't that interested. Some lads he knew couldn't think of anything else. It'll come. When you're ready. Don't worry about it. That's what Taidi would have said. If he'd had time.

They rolled past an alley. Two hollow cheeked men were smoking. Their slitted eyes followed the traffic, as though it was entertainment, or prey. One gave something to the other, who stuffed it in his jeans pocket. The light glinted off the sea between the houses.

Taidi, before he got ill, had taken him to South Stack. They'd sat all afternoon watching guillemots, razorbills, kittiwakes and fulmars. No puffins. They're all out on the sea this time of year, Taidi said. Lucky buggers, that's where I'd be if I could. The lighthouse stuck up into the sky like a thermometer measuring the chill of the evening. Taidi scowled off at the brassy sunset as though he wanted to peer over the horizon. Freedom. No relatives hanging off you like leeches. Just you and your job and your mates. Blokes you might hate like sin but you could trust with your life. Taidi had taken stuff all over the world from Wales (rocks, steel, fertiliser), and brought different stuff back (wood, toys, raincoats). That's how it works, Kye, that's what makes the world go round. That and a bit of wicky-wicky now and again. Kyle had thought about the big ships pushing the world round as they ploughed through the water bringing things they didn't have in Wales. Like raincoats and wicky-wicky.

He had his bird books. He downloaded bird information off websites. But he didn't have Taidi anymore. He'd been worried he wouldn't be able to cry at the funeral, but he knew he only had to think about that and tears would come. He'd written a piece of news about Taidi for school. If they asked him to read it out at assembly he'd have to say he had a sore throat. Because he couldn't read it aloud *without* crying.

Back at the Home they had a buffet. There was Coke for the kids and wine and sherry and whisky for the adults. His cousins were there, trying to get some wine. He hadn't seen them at the crematorium. Maybe they sat at the back. Like they probably did at High School.

"Why don't you go and talk to them instead of moping around with all the old fogeys? Tell them their Aunty Lynn said they have to look after you. And take those sunglasses off. People will think you're blind."

They were hanging round the back of the kitchens by the big bins, smoking. They hid their cigarettes behind their backs when they heard him but brought them out again when they saw who it was.

"Alright Kye? Cool shades." That was Anthony, the oldest. Like Taidi he had tattoos. Only Anthony had never been to sea. He worked part-time in a shoe shop.

Grant asked him if he wanted a drag, offering the stub at arm's length, squinting, holding the smoke in his pigeon chest like the fizz in a bottle.

Leah laughed. He probably hated her most. She was pretty but she was mean.

He went back inside and found his Dad in a circle of men standing drinking whisky from cut glass tumblers. His Dad ruffled his hair. His Uncle Maelor budged up to let him in the circle.

"Have some cake, Kye. Your Aunty Meira made it. Don't he look like his Taid though Merv?"

His Dad grunted. He'd made a speech, saying nice things as though Taidi could hear him inside the coffin. But he never looked like crying. Kyle thought the Aunties on the bench in front of him were sniffling, but when he listened they were whispering about the quiche. His Mum just sat gently drumming her fingers on the red velvet cushion. Taidi wasn't her Dad.

He went to the toilet. There was a red cord hanging over it which he nearly pulled, then he read the warning taped above the cistern. He imagined people in uniforms running, bursting open the door. Him with his pants not quite pulled up.

When he got back he hovered by the puddings, wondering if he could help himself to Aunty Meira's trifle. His Mum's voice carried from across the room, talking to Uncle Maelor.

"He wrote this little piece for school, all about how his Taid used to take him bird watching. It was very sweet. But, well, he only took him the once, when his sailor pal was staying over in the caravan. They probably saw more pink elephants than seagulls."

"You don't have to tell me Lynn. What the Home didn't take he's poured down his throat. All that visiting and you end up with nothing, not even a thank you."

His Mum laughed. "He used to time us in and out! He'd this talking alarm clock with a speech impediment. He made it call the time out when we got there and when we left. Making sure he got his due. *It's three pee ell ... It's seven pee ell ... "*

Taidi's Big Party

Kyle dug into the trifle, lava flows of jelly, custard and cream slurping into the paper bowl. There was sherry in the sponge at the bottom. He wanted to eat so much he'd be drunk from it, then sick all over her on the way home.

***

The week he started High School, Lynn made Kyle help sort Taidi's belongings, to take his mind off being a misfit with no friends. The room at the Home was stuffy, the sun beating in off the flags outside and bumble bees bouncing off the windows as they harvested the lavender.

They had done the outlaw stuff; the leather waistcoat, the cowboy boots, the Confederate bandanas, and in a drawer the revolver which she flung into the fishpond despite Kyle's anguish. Then there was the sailor stuff; a paint spattered short wave radio, a ship in a bottle, some rum miniatures. No letters or postcards. She picked up the alarm clock, not thinking.

It was four-fifteen pee ell.

And then she knew he'd not been getting his money's worth, he'd been counting the seconds till they left him alone. She took Kyle's hand but he pulled it away and hid it behind his back. Tears rolled down her face and dripped onto the clock's face. She smeared them away with her thumb. But to her fury they kept on coming.

THE ADVENTURES OF HIM AND HER

Hannah Riordan

1.
Public transport played a large part in most of his worst nightmares. Buses ranked only second to the London Underground on his list of things he would rather walk than suffer. But that day – sometime in October – he found himself nearly twenty miles from home with not enough cash to afford a taxi and rain heavy enough to leach the colour from the world.

And for those reasons he found himself sitting next to a blurry window, the seat giving a sad squelch as he sat down and that *really* didn't bear thinking about. He flexed his fingers – leather gloves, a self Christmas present from three years back – and tried to think about something that wasn't the grime on the seat and what it must be doing to his coat. He took stock of everyone else on the bus.

Right at the back – the student couple, the boy wearing glasses with no lenses and the girl wearing argyle tights. They probably studied media or photography or some shit like that. The old woman, four rows in front of them. At the front, young mum and infant. The infant was wearing pink and screaming like a TV chef and the mum hardly looked any older than the students at the back. The homeless girl opposite him paid the fare with change fished from a fountain and wore a hoodie that had probably been stolen from around someone's waist at a concert. She had fingerless gloves and the start of a tattoo on her exposed fingers.

Everything about her offended his sense of taste; the purple hair, shaved above one ear and not brushed for weeks. Piercings. Week-old eyeliner. Her boots were on the seat. She saw him looking and grinned, moved over and stuck out a hand.

"I'm Lottie."

It must have been a moment of acute insanity. The same inevitability that had got him on a bus made him smile back. He was wearing gloves, so shaking her hand didn't bother him nearly as much as it should have. "Mark."

2.
It was a couple of days later, when he was driving home from an anticlimactic emergency call-out. He recognised the hair, the hoodie, the army boots. She had a thumb cocked in the direction he was driving and he thought that it made sense to at least *offer* a lift.

She slammed the door hard enough to make him worry about the glass.

"Where do you want dropping?" He tried to sound calm enough as she put her seatbelt on and he wondered if it was possible for damp hair dye to soak into the seat covers.

"Huh? Oh, wherever. I'm going to the Cross Keys down on Bell End, but wherever's closest really."

It made him pause, because he had never heard of anywhere local called Bell End.

"Do you mean Bell Lane?" She didn't, because Bell Lane was one of those suburban streets, all pale brick and pruned gardens.

She quirked an eyebrow. "Bellegrade."

That made more sense, so he nodded and took the third exit. It was a good fifteen minutes out of his way.

3.

It quickly became a thing. Because, as he discovered, Lottie walked everywhere and hitched about 90% of the time and wanted to go everywhere, bumming around at concerts with free entry and people she maybe vaguely knew.

When he first realised that her food intake was erratic at best, he started pulling in at the drive-through and getting burgers. She had calmly informed him that she didn't fuck for chips and then asked if she could smoke in his car. He'd said no, but she'd done it anyway, head and arm mostly out the window.

"Keep doing that and you'll be walking." It was an empty threat and it made her laugh.

"You'd miss me too much."

He wasn't sure if he was more worried that she was right, or that she was getting cigarette ash on his floor.

They saw the first snow of the year in late November and when she pulled a joint out from her pocket and moved to light it he said no.

"Come on, man. It's fucking freezing and this is the only jumper I got."

"Cigarettes are one thing, Lott, but this is crossing the line."

"Fuck you." But she put it away and he felt the tightness in his chest ease up.

"Where do you want dropping?"

"Queen's Park. Nothing else going on; just need somewhere to catch a few hours."

Before he could stop his mouth he was offering his sofa as somewhere to sleep and she looked bemused, but shrugged anyway.

"Why not."

4.

He had several very good reasons "why not", but afterwards it never seemed to matter much. She came and went as she pleased and didn't question why she shouldn't move things or why the house always smelt like bleach and Dettol.

Mud ended up on the carpet on several occasions, but it was her, just the sort of person she was, and he didn't feel like he wanted to scrub that out of the fibres.

It was only in March when he realised that she had become a strange unpredictable constant in his world of carefully scheduled routine and by then she penned things in his diary like "film night" and "super-purple-porn reading". The former involved take-out and rented movies. The latter involved Mills and Boon novels purchased for pennies in charity shops and read out loud until they were both laughing so hard they couldn't stand up.

They talked a lot. He explained the basics of economics to her and had reached micro- and macro-economic theory when she started snoring. He learnt that she had a university place at one point but got kicked out and that she was *mostly* clean. She prodded until he produced the photo album and went quiet when she found the ones of his ex-girlfriend. He learnt the hard way that their music tastes were not, and could never be, compatible.

5.
It ended in July because she left. No note. She didn't take anything with her; he just got in from work to find her absence.

He cleaned the carpet, then the bathroom and broke down while doing the tiles – sobbed over a bucket of bleach and water until his face felt raw.

6.
She appeared in his life twice in the next year. Once in a newspaper, in the background of a photo that accompanied a piece about festival riots. A picture in profile; the familiar but ridiculous hairstyle and the tattoos on her shoulder. The second time was in the

street. She walked past him and for a second she was close enough to touch but she didn't see him, kept walking, and by the time he was opening his mouth to say something she was already gone.

His diary, his house, his carpet were still organised. The Mills and Boon books were in a labelled box in his wardrobe.

7.
She showed up in January. Breathing into her hands as she stood outside his door and shifting her weight from one foot to another. She'd lost at least three of the piercings he could see and her hair had been re-dyed blue.

He didn't even know where to start, so he just sat at his own table keeping his breathing steady while she made tea.

"I'm clean now," she said eventually to break the silence. "Got on one of the support schemes. Going to uni in September." She hissed when she splashed boiling water on her thumb and sucked it.

"Put it under the cold tap." He said. The streetlamps outside reflected themselves in the metal and the water and he wanted to ask where she'd been, but he already knew. Festivals, rehab, getting better and worse and, eventually, getting here. He knew she was looking around too, looking for anything that would indicate change.

"What did you do with my books?" She said as she pulled her thumb back, water still thundering into the sink, examined the pink mark. "You didn't throw them out, did you?"

That at least made him smile. "No, no. They're around."

To which, all she seemed to be able to say was, "Cool. Happy New Year for last week, by the way."

Later, he put on one of his box sets of American crime dramas, and she went to the toilet and came back with her box of romance novels and his favourite Indian take-out menu. There was mud on the carpet where it had fallen off her jeans and she'd spilt tea on his diary when she took it out to look. She'd mopped it up with kitchen roll, and the lines on the paper fuzzed and the words were rendered unreadable.

THE INHERITANCE

Sophie Green

Albert
The Goldsteins had always been extraordinary.

From his grandfather Albert's portrait, Francis knew that he had inherited his glassy blue eyes and thin pale hair, which Albert had worn oiled and combed back emphasising his bulb-shaped head.

They had all heard the story. Albert met Mae, the love of his life, in Paris, among the perfume of tobacco and aniseed. Albert was three feet seven inches tall. He made his living as a crooner in a candlelit night spot in Pigalle. His silvery voice weaved between the tables like a spell. In between songs he told comical anecdotes and sometimes he had special guests. Once he was on the radio.

Mae Bloom fell in love straightaway. In those days Mae was a mind reader. Her most notable feature was then – and would always be – her lustrous black hair which she wore in two coils, one piled high and flopped over her left brow like a shiny black beret, the other hung loose over her left shoulder. She had strong fingers on fat hands. She liked gold and wore her riches in bracelets and rings.

The two lovers escaped France at the beginning of the occupation and came to England. Albert was too small to enlist but he was given an unofficial posting entertaining the troops at RAF Beachy Head.

In 1944 he had been awarded the George Cross for "most conspicuous courage in circumstances of extreme danger". He had distinguished himself in the daring rescue of an American pilot from a burning plane which had become lodged in a Scots pine during a training exercise.

Francis often pondered the portrait of his grandfather, which now rested atop his grandmother's dressing table in an ornate brass frame. Albert was dressed in a thick green uniform and military cap, with the George Cross pinned to his chest. He was in soft focus like a forces' sweetheart. It was a rejected still from publicity shots taken for his act; in this one it was considered that he looked too grave, too doe-eyed and sincere for a comedy act. He looked like a film star.

Francis's grandfather had been extraordinary, there was no doubt.

Edward
After the war, they had joined the circus. They lived on site in the painted caravan that Mae used for her act. It was fitted with honey-coloured wooden sideboards and foldaway tables, clever hinges and secret cupboards and decorated with painted tin plates and picture frames.

There is a picture of Albert sitting on the steps of their caravan cradling his first and only child,

Edward, across his knees like a huge doll. The baby's face is blurred by a sudden movement. They are surrounded by a haze of fine dust and drifting insects in the slanting early light. It's the only image Francis has seen that ties the two men together.

Edward lost his father just before he turned nine. When one of the circus lions, enraged by hunger and cabin fever, cornered his trainer in the travelling cage, it was Albert who briskly took off his right shoe and hurled it at the beast to draw him off. The lion had closed his jaws around Albert's neck and lifted him off the ground, muffling any screams there might have been inside his huge mouth. He paced back and forth before the crowd with Albert's twitching body hanging from his mouth.

After several terrible seconds there came a crack which split the sky and a tang of smoke in the air. The small body went limp. The second shot felled the lion.

Edward was not sure whether or not he really remembered this or he has been told the story so many times that he thought he was there.

Mae never recovered from the loss. She closed up the van and kept Edward out of school. Her grief bound tight around them both like a shroud.

In his teens, Edward, who had always been thin, became suddenly very tall; his arms and legs grew more spindly as they became longer, until he resembled nothing so much as a crane fly, brittle, transitory and irritating to be around.

Lost and Found

The caravan was now too small for them both to live happily in and so Mae signed up for a council house and a few months later they were living on the outskirts of Bournemouth. Mae decorated the house with posters and pictures of her late husband, until he filled every room; he was present at every meal time. He even watched over Edward while he slept, from his post on the landing wall.

Edward could not have been more different from his parents, but as it was he too turned out to be extraordinary.

Francis had seen his father's name on the flyer for a Spectacular! at the Pavilion Theatre. They called him Edward the Astounding. Even out of season his magic show topped the hotel entertainment bill every Thursday night. Mae said the crowds watched him with a sense of terrified wonderment, transfixed by his speed, magnetism and charisma as he fanned cards, unknotted silk ropes and made his assistant vanish and reappear. His fingers moved like hummingbirds, his spindly arms tucked tidily away in the sleeves of his smart work tuxedo, leaving space enough to hide an array of doves, rabbits, coloured handkerchiefs, flowers and coins.

Francis had only ever seen his father perform tricks at the kitchen table, and once at a birthday party. By the time Francis was born, Edward the Astounding Magician had been replaced by Edward the Chartered Accountant, but as Mae described the performance he could imagine the silent anticipation of the onlookers, the startled disbelief, and unnerved giggles that must have followed the big reveal. When Francis pictures this scene his father's eyes gleam.

Edward met and married Caroline, whose father owned a kiosk hung with beach balls and castle-shaped buckets. She moved into the house and they seemed to live happily in this way, at first, and if the enchantment of being in love wore off, a different sort of bond replaced it. Caroline gave birth to two beautiful boys; Louis, and then, two years later, Francis.

Francis
Louis was extraordinary, although even he had gone through an anxious few years when, at eleven, he exceeded the height of his beloved grandfather as it was mapped on the wall. That year, the line was drawn with thinner pencil, like a disappointed thread. Luckily for him he had stopped growing soon after and remained at four foot.

Francis clearly took after his father, tall and stringy, pale and quiet. He didn't seek out attention, but somehow, Louis noticed, he still got it. Because Francis, in his own understated way, was also extraordinary.

Unfortunately for Francis, Mae had told him that his own extraordinary ability manifested itself in a quiet way, when he was alone and no one could see.

Francis never levitated in a conscious state, so he, like the rest of his family, had only his grandmother's word that he could. She told stories of how he used to rise out of his cot as a baby. She told him how they had to make a tepee from a net curtain, to hang over his cot like a bivouac to stop him floating into danger. Francis doesn't remember this at all although he does recall the sensation of a suffocating blur surrounding him. He can imagine how it would feel to rise in the air, as if through water, feeling it flow around him and then the sudden shock of falling, the breathlessness as gravity pulls him down, the hardness of an unyielding floorboard against bony shoulder blades. But this could not be real; the floor of his own bedroom, the only place he had ever slept, was covered in rugs.

Weighed down by his own expectations, Francis lay on his narrow bed and tried to imagine weightlessness, the ceiling growing near, a cushion of air below him. Sometimes, with a feigned lack of consciousness, he would raise his arms and legs off the bed, but his body would anchor him to the counterpane.

He couldn't convince himself. In his heart he knew that his only extraordinary quality was that in a family such as his, he was ordinary. In fact, had it not been that Francis had Albert's eyes and receding hairline he might not have been a Goldstein at all.

When she couldn't sleep, Mae would sit out in the garden on the flimsy swing, which wheezed and creaked as she drifted back and forth in the early hours of the morning. She sat, crocheting with wool that was dyed in rich hues. She looked up at the room where Francis slept and, seeing the curtains flutter and suck inwards as the gangly shadow rose, hoped he had remembered to lock the window.

17 HOURS ACROSS STATE

Barbara Corfield

Joseph's report read "an imaginative and energetic boy". He was bored of school and raced to learn from the study of snails and the bounciness of silly putty. His entertainment was a knight's sword cut from the branch of the highest tree, a pirate's patch made of the finest sycamore leaf. A good dinner would have burst the seams of his grey school shorts. His many adventures were evident in the pulls on his jumper and the bruises on his legs. At the weekend he never lingered in bed as his own internal clock chimed into action. Having no siblings allowed him freedom to roam the house like a spy, stealing around walls, peeping through steamed-up, crumbling windows. His parents lived with his Grandmother in a wooden, picket fenced house, stereotypically whitewashed, with two chairs on the porch, and a fly-screen door.

Nine-year-old Joseph loved to sit with his Nana listening to her stories of magic mirrors and faraway kingdoms, unaware of her faint smell of cigars and soup-stained bosom. It was 1983, and little Joseph had run home, the entire length of Oakley, before hanging a right into Poplar Avenue, his face red as a summer berry. In his hand he clutched a puppet, a policeman with a cotton ball pom-pom nose and green eyes. All day Joseph smiled about the show he would perform that evening on the porch rail. As he rounded the corner his legs slowed and his eyes widened, he didn't know why there were so many cars or so many people, but he could see his Nana's slippers, one on the porch and one on the grassy verge. A blur of seventy-two hours full of strangers, being sent to his room, eating left over sandwiches and a house full of flowers followed. The puppet never left his blazer pocket. Five weeks later the cases were packed and they shipped out to Michigan leaving the white picket fence memories and the smell of stewed apples behind.

Twenty-seven years had little extra to show on his frame. Joseph eyed himself up and down in the hall mirror, playing with the pulled cotton on his sleeve trying to push it back in with his finger-nail. "Look out below, me hearties!" A momentary yelp before he was landed upon by a flying flash of red cape.

"For God's sake, Sam, you nearly killed me."

Sam, pulling himself up to his entire three feet ten inches sighed, "Dad, when are you gonna learn to move quicker?" Joseph's adult life was a far cry from the clean-aired childhood he had spent on the porch. In Michigan, his Father had got a job in the Automotive business, his Mother in the local store whilst Joseph has passed his years spinning dimes on the pavement. His College sweetheart had fallen for his boyish looks and his early marriage proposal. Money was tight, especially when Sam arrived, but they held together. On 21 August an invitation fell on the mat; it had been forwarded by his Mother with a sticky-note attached:

Hope you can come to this. Me and your Father are going to try and make it. It would be lovely to see the area again. x

The invitation was for a neighbour of his late Grandmother. It was her eightieth birthday, an achievement being marked by a street party.

"Please, oh pleeeeeease can we go?" Sam pleaded. He had never been in a street where you could play, let alone have a party in. On ninety-fourth between first and second, the apartment that the family shared cast shadows on the pavement below. The buzzer downstairs didn't work, so visitors would holler loudly from the roadside until, at best they were noticed, or at worst were soaked by water thrown from an open window above. Joseph would love his son to taste his own childhood, and considering they hadn't had a vacation in the six years since Sam was born, they were deserving of the fresh air that this trip would bring. After negotiating with the landlord over rent day, and making many empty promises to workmates to work their next weekend shift if they covered for a few days, they packed up the battered sedan and left, driving across state some seventeen hours.

2 am. With his wife in the passenger seat, and young son strapped in the back Joseph felt safe; he was half

way through the journey, closer to his past than to the present. The car lights cut through the slick oil night, the sounds of the ghost-like trees rushed past the windows imitating the heavy breathing of his two beautiful passengers. With little stimulus other than lines on the road, he enveloped himself in childhood memories. On his eighth birthday, he received a whittling knife and a thick branch from a man who lived along the road, he sat in the garden for two hours that evening, oblivious to the balloons, leftover cake and presents he had received. His Mother had commented that she had never seen him sit for so long in one place. Picking away with the knife, chipping and smoothing the branch, distorting its shape until, with sore fingers he ran into the house. His Grandmother had smiled as he showed her the carved object, a little wooden car, and a very good little car. "You have a talent there," she had whispered, "Now put it extra safe in a secret place." He could not remember where he had put the little car, nor did it matter much now, but the memory made his heart heavy. He brushed a single tear away with his sleeve just as an articulated lorry hissed past. Now, with aching shoulders and a headache he pulled the car to the side of the road, to stare at his family, and whispered, "I'm sorry, I let you both down."

11 am, a sunny Saturday morning. The traffic lights changed for the second time.

"Come on, Joe. It'll be just fine," his wife eagerly encouraging him to drive the last few hundred yards to their destination. The roads were surprisingly clear, no pedestrians bustling past each other invading each other's space, clutching bags as though their lives depended upon their contents.

"It's just been a while," he muttered.

"I know, but Sam's really looking forward to it. Your folks will be there already, we'll look for them, eh?"

Turning into Oakley his eyes widened, "God, nothing has changed, it's just the same. Look – the bottle tree, I nicknamed it that because the tree stump had a hole in the middle just big enough to put a glass bottle of lemonade in. Do you see it, Sam, out of your window?" Managing to break a smile, he rolled to a halt.

An entire Avenue, about forty homes all whitewash and picket fences, lined the street, eager to look the prettiest. Each house had yellow ribbons tied to the porch rails. Tables ran the length of the street, uneven heights, pulled from the corners of people's garages. Fold-out wooden tables, plastic garden and dining tables, different legs showing under their white paper coverings. Each table top was laid around a bowl of sunshine carnations, with plates of all sizes and colours, snacks peeping out from their cling wrap covers, and in the air, the smell of ageing perfume and piecrust. Joseph's parents had proudly showed off Sam, introducing him as their "cheeky little grandson" while the young couple from Michigan were overwhelmed by people's hospitality. Their eighty-year-old hostess (who would never have passed for a day over sixty) had insisted they stayed in her annexe rather than some motel.

As the day closed, Joseph sat on the front porch. From his chair, he could watch his son picking cake crumbs off the table tops with the other children, hearing how many words they could think of to rhyme with pie. His Grandmother's old house was now bustling with activity, two twin boy-scouts and their twelve-week-old spaniel. Joseph's wife joined him on the porch. Looking at his face, she didn't need to ask what he was thinking.

"We have each other. That's all that matters." She wrapped her arms around his shoulders. He was shivering.

They sat together, pretending it was real, late into the night. Long after Sam was carried to bed, the paper table coverings fluttered and the clouds fell. Joseph, now driven by fear of the coming morning and the journey back to Michigan, could hear nothing but the beating in his chest, and ringing in his ears. Either of the two could have said it, but only Joseph was honest enough.

"Yesterday is dead," he whispered, "but our little family is not. We're not going back."

PART OF THE FURNITURE

Richard Lakin

They gave him a card. *Sorry You're Leaving,* it said. He picked up the box containing the things he'd accumulated over the years. There was a hole-punch, a coffee-stained dictionary, a chipped mug, a Flying Scotsman mouse mat, teabags in foil and half a pack of custard creams. Norman glanced back at his desk. The only trace of his twenty-two years in procurement was a "Visit Wales" sticker clinging stubbornly to his monitor.

"Bye then, Norman," Carole Fish trilled.

"Yes, good luck matey," Trevor Boon said.

Norman raised a hand as he strolled through the door. They were delighted he hadn't suggested a drink. He couldn't think of anything worse than Scotch eggs, gassy lager and a forced silence at the Poacher's Cottage. He'd gone quietly, which was best for everyone.

Norman thought he was due a spot of daydreaming or a crossword or two after all those years paying tax, but the government had different ideas. When he signed on he was told to attend a group called Quest. The group was run by Nikki – two 'k's and two 'i's. Nikki clicked her pen incessantly, when she wasn't smoothing her skirt across her knees.

Part of the Furniture

She fixed Norman up with a badge. It said *Norman Hancock, Job Hunter!* She asked him to tell the others about himself and what he wanted from Quest. *No pressure, no rush, Norm.*

Norman said he wanted a job. He was terrified of a future that promised afternoons watching daytime TV, crumpled betting slips and Happy Hours beginning at breakfast. So when Nikki offered him the post at Squirrel's Leap he took it, although he knew he could do better.

"They're lovely people," Nikki beamed, "look on it as a foot on the ladder." She phoned for a taxi, her shocking pink nails clinking like porcelain on the keys. "No time like the present, Norm," she said.

Norman didn't think she got many of her *Job Hunters!* into work. She walked him to the taxi, probably making sure.

That was three weeks ago and Norman was already "part of the furniture" according to Matron. The ammonia-stench of wet sheets and bedpans and the seep of boiling cabbage and swede got everywhere, but Squirrel's Leap was a cheery enough place. It was hard work and Norman quickly learned to mouth-breathe, but there were benefits. He liked being on his feet because the time passed quicker. He was given plants to tend in reception and he got to go on outings to garden centres and stately homes.

Most Wednesdays they had singing in the conservatory, or "orangery", as Matron called it. Norman would play his harmonica and when Matron wasn't about he'd tell the residents the only oranges they'd find at Squirrel's Leap came from Tesco. Millie and Flo chuckled at that, so Norman made a thing of telling jokes before Mrs Horncastle played "Roll out the Barrel" on the piano. On Fridays he brought in Patsy Cline and Pat Boone albums for them. For the first time in his life Norman felt sure he was making a difference.

He was sipping tea, flicking through Muriel's *People's Friend*, when Matron came into the staff room.

"We've had a new addition," she said.

"We're getting too popular," Norman replied.

"Her name's Octavia." Matron tried a cut-glass accent. "Take her a cuppa and give her a bit of your chat."

Norman nodded. He knew what Matron said about him. *Norman's got the gift of the gab with the old dears. Shame he can't find someone his own age.*

Octavia sat in an armchair picking at her pink cardigan. Norman set two mugs down on coasters.

"Do you take?"

Octavia frowned. Then she saw he was indicating sugar and shook her head.

"Quite right," Norman said, "a moment on the lips, a lifetime on the hips, eh?"

Octavia shuffled in the armchair, irritated by squeaks from the plastic cover.

"Are the armchairs all like this?" she said.

"I can get it removed, if you like."

"Yes, please," she said.

Norman sipped his tea. Octavia opened a cardboard box and took out a tin. She popped the lid and held it close to her chest.

"I'm fine," she said, "so if you've got something you need to do ..."

"Exit stage left," Norman quipped.

Octavia turned her back, dismissing him. She set a porcelain figurine on the windowsill, turning it until she was happy with the light. She took a framed photo from the tin. Norman paused in the doorway. She had her back to him, but he saw her stroke the photograph with a fingertip. He closed the door silently.

Later, when Norman had given the reception area and toilets a good going over, he decided to look in on Octavia. He liked to keep an eye on the new ones, helping them to settle in. Octavia had hardly touched her fish in white wine sauce, but she'd eaten an almond slice and stayed with the others to watch the regional weather.

He tapped on Octavia's door, but there was no answer. The door was ajar, so he poked his head in. The room smelt of lavender and furniture polish. Here was a woman with standards to keep up, Norman thought. Perhaps Octavia had joined in the bingo with the others. He doubted it.

Norman picked up her cardigan, where it had been draped on the armchair, and folded it. He was staring out of the window – enjoying a precious bit of *me time*, Matron called it – when the framed photograph caught his eye. It was a wedding photo.

The bride had the same heart-shaped face. It was Octavia, blushing under a drift of confetti, preparing to throw her bouquet. Norman's heart thudded in his chest. He swayed and had to grab at the windowsill. When he had steadied himself, he swallowed, dry-mouthed, and picked up the photograph. There was a roaring in his ears; the same roar he remembered from walking the top diving board as a schoolboy. Octavia made a beautiful bride, but it was the groom Norman stared at. He sat on Octavia's bed, kneading his forehead with the heel of his hand.

Norman didn't resign, didn't tell anyone he was leaving. He fetched his coat, pushing his arms into the sleeves as he jogged down the drive. The frame banged against his ribs as he hurried on, breathless. He turned the key in the back door. The radio was on low, eggs spattered in the pan.

"You're early," Mum said. "I thought you were working a late."

Norman didn't answer.

"Do you want tea?"

He shook his head.

"Is something wrong?"

Norman slammed the door behind him.

Jack was staring into a greasy pint pot, clouded with thumbprints. He downed the last of his mild and called for another. Brenda was pouring when Norman slammed the photograph on the bar. The frame shattered and a hairline crack ran through the glass.

"I don't want any bother," Brenda said.

"When was this?" Norman asked.

Jack picked up his pint, blew the froth from the top, and sank half of it. Norman's fists bunched, his toenails bit into his soles.

"That'd be 1968," Jack said, without glancing at the photo.

Norman blinked. "And I'd be what, seven?" he said.

Jack shrugged.

"Some bloody father you are," he spat.

Jack's eyes were like slits.

"You broke the law," Norman said. "You go to jail for bigamy."

"She's in your place, isn't she?" Jack said. "She's losing her marbles, you know. You'll do no one any favours raking stuff up."

Jack kept a lorry for years. He was often away on deliveries. Norman thought of all those Christmases when Jack was late, all the bank holiday runs to Hull or Liverpool.

"How long did it go on for?" he said.

"Does it matter?" Jack said.

Norman stuck the photo in his jacket.

"What'll you do?" Jack said. He rubbed the bristles on his chin, but when he glanced up at the mirror on the bar he saw Norman had gone.

"Pour us another, Bren," he said.

Mum was at bingo. Norman left her daffodils, her favourite, soaking in the sink. He slipped back into Squirrel's Leap, relieved to see Matron was out. He told the others he was sorry, he owed them one. He tapped Octavia's door and went in.

"I owe you an apology," he said.

She was reading a paperback.

"I was dusting when I knocked this over and broke the frame."

She took it from him, smiled.

"I got you a new one."

Octavia set it down on the windowsill. She stared out of the window. "You remind me," she said, tapping the photo with her fingertip.

"Nothing like him," Norman said, under his breath.

THE LIBRARY

Sarah Leigh

The car was like a kiln. Frank's trousers felt sticky against the scuffed leather seat. He hoped it was just sweat. He looked for a handle to wind the window down but found only buttons.

"How does this open?"

"Don't. Touch. Anything." His wife's words punctured him like pins. After fifty years of marriage Vera was no longer a wife, she was more like a, like a … what? He imagined a dark castle, twists of barbed wire. Yes. A Kommandant at Colditz. Cold. She restrained him.

His window magically lowered. Vera must have done it. He definitely hadn't touched anything. The air rushed in, smelling of melted tarmac, as hot as the air inside, blowing over his scalp, drying the sheen of sweat. He should have had that thing fitted – that cooling thing – he couldn't remember the name. But the car was decaying now, not worth the expense.

They reached the brow of a hill. The town dwindled behind them and the view before them opened up. Away to the right, two tall white chimneys loomed over other, smaller ones. White vapours billowed into the sky above an assortment of rectangular structures – some grey, some newly white, others green and rusting. Off to the left, the grimy chemical factory stood desolately by the banks of the river Weaver. Frank felt the warm seep of nostalgia. This was where he'd worked. They were going past his old office.

The road straightened and he saw the rise of the iron bridge, the familiar beige bricks. Vera swung into Solvay Road, driving past the wide frontage of the Mond Building. He'd still been young when he started here: a frenzy of energy, joking, speeding in on his old Norton, his wiry hair blown to a quiff in the wind. The old feelings were still there. Wait – something wasn't right. No cars parked at the front. The entrance doors shut tight. One of the windows had a notice saying "Sauna Sauna". Was that two saunas? Or did it mean something else? Buried among the overgrown shrubs at the front was the old sign proclaiming "ICI Chemicals and Polymers". But where was everyone?

He remembered striding in through those doors, briefcase in hand, bounding up the stairs and along a high-ceilinged corridor down to the library. His library. Three members of staff he'd been in charge of: his domain. Inside were carpets and wood-panelled walls, soaking up muffled whispers. He remembered the cloying smell of musty paper, the satisfying clunk of the heavy date stamp. Was all that still going on inside, right now?

"What are we doing here?" he asked.

Vera forced a loud sigh. "I've told you three times. We're picking up Jasmine."

Frank tried to remember working with someone called Jasmine. No one came to mind. "Who's Jasmine?"

"For heaven's sake, Frank. Your granddaughter."

"Oh. Yes." That Jasmine.

Vera drove around the back of the building, his old office building, and parked. It seemed all wrong. This was the back entrance.

"But what is she doing here?"

"She's been to a party."

"A party? At ICI?"

"It's not ICI any more. It was bought out, years ago."

"But I saw the sign."

Vera took the key out of the ignition. "You're imagining things."

"No I'm not."

"Well anyway, sign or no sign, it's not ICI any more. Are you coming?" She unfastened his seat belt causing the buckle to ping into his ribs.

They passed two industrial-size bins and entered through what should have been the post room. The corridor was black with garish blue and orange carpet. Pop music blared as they pushed through a swing door. Frank had never understood pop music. He blinked in the bright lights amid a clatter of bowling skittles. There was a young girl running around in a shiny purple dress. Frank could smell sweaty shoes. A young lad at a table was devouring a charred-looking burger, ketchup smeared around his mouth. Two boys wielded plastic weapons at a video screen, machine gun stutters droning out. The whole scene disturbed him. Could his granddaughter really be enjoying herself in this place? How on earth had this been allowed to happen here, in the ICI offices? He couldn't understand it.

"Stay here," said Vera, gripping his arm hard and pushing him towards a chair. "I'm going to find her. Don't move." She went towards the bowling lanes and seemed to dissolve amongst the people.

Frank sat on the plastic chair uneasily. He saw a pink foil balloon stuck on the ceiling pipes. *Happy Birthday!* it proclaimed, bobbing around, looking like it was trying to find a way out. He thought of the library again. The tall rows of quiet shelves, so close you couldn't pass anyone, the mahogany steps on wheels, Beryl the assistant going up them, dutifully, doing anything Frank asked her to do. He was in charge. He remembered she had round, dimpled knees and dough-white skin. But her calves were fat, although that hadn't stopped him imagining how it might feel to slide his hand over them. Or perhaps he really had. Sometimes things he thought he'd dreamed turned out to be real, and vice versa. His brain was a Swiss cheese. He was living on shifting sand, each wave of memory fresh and glittering for an instant before being obliterated.

He stood and walked towards the toilets. Vera couldn't stop him going for a pee if he needed one. Next to the gents' was a door marked *Private*. He hovered. He knew he shouldn't, but he tried the handle. Miraculously, it gave, and Frank slipped through unnoticed into an unlit corridor.

The door clicked shut and it was quiet. There was light ahead, no carpet, the ground sloping gently upwards. Around a corner he found a stairwell. His shoes echoed as he went up. The sun forced its way through dusty panes of glass, warming his scalp. On the first floor he had to push hard to get through the sticking door but then there he was, on the old corridor. How many times had he walked down here? He felt excited now, striding towards his library. He passed an office with a brass nameplate: *Harold Edgeley*, but the man was forgotten to him. A distant door banged, then he heard whispering and a woman's laugh – short, and high-pitched, followed by a clunk. Then, nothing. There were still people here. He pushed on.

The library door had lost its sign but he recognised the ornate brass handle. It turned smoothly. He hesitated a second before entering, breathing in the musty smell. Inside, the room seemed vast and desolate: no books, no shelves, nothing. Frank walked across bare floorboards to the far side where his desk had stood. Even the carpet had been stripped. But there was the huge window, the very one he'd sat and stared out of for forty-two years. The glass was daubed with white-out. He lifted the familiar latch and pushed but it wouldn't budge. He really wanted to get it open, to see the old view again.

He shoved his shoulder against the glass. Then he banged it with the heel of his hand, loosening it all around. There was a lot of rust. Flakes of burnt orange scattered at his feet. He went on tip-toe for the top edge and gave another almighty shove, nearly losing his balance. Finally it opened, enough to see a chestnut tree and weeping willows by the river, the view, his view, still there. Frank inhaled the fresh air, heard the water gurgling over the weir.

"I might have known." Vera's voice made him jump.

"Granddad!" Jasmine ran towards him, smiling.

"I told you to stay put."

"I just wanted to see the old place again," said Frank. He leaned down towards his granddaughter. "Granddad used to work here."

Jasmine grabbed his hand. "Don't be silly, Granddad, there's nothing here. Just a poky old smelly building." She pulled him away. He took one last look.

Later, as they drove off, Frank tried to spot the still-open window.

"Slow down a minute," he said. But Vera accelerated, and he couldn't find it. They travelled home in silence. Jasmine ate her sweets and Frank turned his head towards the open window, letting the wind buffet his damp cheeks.

SMALL ACCOMMODATIONS

Angi Holden

"It's a buyers' market," said the estate agent, tossing a sheaf of papers across the desk. "Take your pick."

David picked them up and leafed through the stapled sheets. If the man was acting on behalf of his clients he wasn't doing a very good job, he thought. He sorted them methodically into three piles: yes, no and maybe. The first pile comprised a single property; there were another half dozen worthy of further consideration but most ended up on the no pile. He gathered up the maybes and glanced through them again, turning the pages thoughtfully as he sipped from the cooling mug of instant coffee.

The top one had a lovely garden, but he planned to spend considerable periods of time travelling. Europe certainly, Canada and New Zealand almost definitely. India perhaps. And although he'd never expressed any particular interest in visiting America, a friend had recommended a coast-to-coast itinerary, which included a train journey through the Rockies. So no garden. It would become a liability. A modern bungalow also ended up on the no pile, along with an awkward barn conversion and a flat which lacked adequate parking.

"I'm interested in those," he told the agent, indicating his selection. "Can you point them out on the map?" A further two were discarded. Twenty minutes later, with four appointments and his satnav armed with postcodes, David was on the way to his first viewing.

In the event, it was hardly a difficult decision. Initially he had a sense of having slipped into one of those property programmes that Marion had taken to watching in the afternoons. *Escape to the Country* or *Location, Location*, where couples – it was always couples he suddenly realised – visited a number of houses of varying degrees of unsuitability. As her strength diminished, she'd become increasing drawn towards properties in need of restoration. She'd spoken of taking on a neglected building, a vicarage perhaps or an abandoned guest house, as though being immersed in its renovation might have given her the motivation to hang on a little longer.

The first property would have appealed to her. The middle-aged woman who came out to meet David introduced herself as a neighbour and apologised for her muddy Wellingtons.

"I was walking the dog when Abbots rang," she said. An old black Labrador was tied loosely to a metal boot scraper by the front door. She had been the old lady's carer, she explained, and had reluctantly agreed to be the key-holder on behalf of the vendor, whom she'd never met. David apologised for interrupting her walk. She let him in, pausing to heave the boots from her stockinged feet. "Follow me," she said as she set off, leaving a trail of moist footprints across the quarry tiles.

It was a decent property, David thought, a sturdy family house that needed love and attention, a house in want of a woman in the kitchen and the squeal of children thundering down the stairs to squabble over who was going to lick out the mixing bowl or bag the largest slice of cake. He saw Marion as she'd been twenty years ago, strands of hair escaping from a tortoiseshell clip, a dab of flour on her cheek, contentment in her eyes. How she might have been, at least.

Out of politeness, he trailed around after the woman whose name he had already forgotten, feigning interest in the original features – barley-twist spindles on the staircase, a carved fire surround – and commenting favourably on the size of rooms that he knew were too large for his needs. He had of course been misled, expecting something more compact for the money, although he now saw that the price reflected the amount of work needed and the urgency of the distant relative to realise the value of a newly acquired asset.

As he drove away, car windows wound down, he played the property show game. His valuation – or since he knew the asking price, his expectation – weighed against the details on the estate agent's paperwork. So far, not so good, he thought. He would need to do better at the next house. He turned up the bass on the radio and headed north.

Lost and Found

The second and third properties were reasonable, but had been flattered by the photographer. Both were located on the kinds of estate he'd grown up on and spent most of his life trying to avoid. Sycamore Grove, Plover Close, Derwent Avenue. "Well-appointed" houses, according to Abbots. He couldn't disagree, although he would have added: bland and characterless, designed by architects who lacked vision and built on roads that always seemed to be named after trees or birds or rivers, as though pastoral titles could mask their urban solidity. Expectation and reality drifted wider apart.

The wildcard – the shows Marion watched always included a wildcard – was much further along the coast than he'd intended looking. Nearer the coast too, so that when he initially saw the image printed on the sheet he'd imagined it to have been converted from the remnants of a lighthouse. He parked on the road and walked up the block-paved driveway. Looking up at the cylindrical building silhouetted against the skyline he saw his mistake. The door opened before he reached the porch, and he was greeted by a slight woman in her early thirties.

"Welcome to The Mill House," she said. She smiled, but there was regret in her expression too. She was sad to be leaving, she told him. David climbed the spiral staircase, peered into odd shaped rooms, gazed out of windows towards the distant sea. He judged that on a good day he could walk as far as the beach and back. On a bad one, he could simply sit in the upstairs lounge and watch the crested waves pounding the shoreline. Read a little, paint. Perhaps plan his next trip – The Mill House would always be waiting when he came back.

He stayed to share a pot of tea with the woman. She and her partner had loved living here, but the accommodation was too small for their needs now – her hand slipped unconsciously to her belly. Extending would be difficult given the shape of the building and anyway, there was insufficient garden. He thought his way into the house, placing the chair he'd inherited from his father by the sea-facing window alongside Marion's favourite rug, deep sapphire and maroon and fringed with blonde tassels. He would visit auctions until he found the right brass bedstead, and a scrubbed oak table for the kitchen. The rest of his furniture could go; he had little need for sideboards and wardrobes with mirrored doors.

As he left he turned to say goodbye to the woman, and thanked her for her hospitality.

"I hope you'll be very happy here," she said, offering her hand as if it had already been agreed.

His house sold quickly, despite the recession. Marion had chosen well, and had decorated and furnished their home with impeccable taste. The buyers made offers for the Chesterfield and the mahogany table and chairs, for the bedroom suite and the made-to-measure curtains. With relief he accepted, neither knowing nor caring whether the sums were reasonable. He spent a week sorting through his books, keeping only his father's Folio editions of Dickens, a selection of reference books and a few favourite novels. The rest, along with Marion's extensive collection of cookery books, went to Oxfam. He packed her clothes, shoes and handbags into cardboard boxes and delivered them to the local hospice shop. Her jewellery – everything except the wedding ring she'd been buried in and the engagement ring which he'd placed in an envelope with their marriage lines – he gave to her Goddaughter.

Even after the move David found he was still discarding things, reducing his possessions to suit his new accommodation. He replaced his computer with a more powerful laptop, his array of photographic equipment with a compact digital camera that he could stuff in his pocket for his walks down to the shore. Marion's collection of creamware, which he'd initially thought might suit the cottage, looked ostentatious; he kept only an oval fruit dish. On the deep stone windowsill, its blue flowers seemed to tremble across the buttery glaze.

Beside the dish he placed fragments of seaglass, a handful of shells, a mermaid's purse, finding that some things, like some people, seemed to fit their space.

WINDOW DRESSING

Lynne Parry-Griffiths

Sometimes she leaves the light on all night, a dull orange glowing through heavy cream-lined curtains. I know they're cream, even though it's the lining that faces outwards, but if you look really closely you can just about make out the edging. Everything about her's classy: car, clothes, bed-linen. That's always white. She hangs it on her rotary line.

    I always watch the weather forecast. When that smiling blonde lady tells me it won't be warm and sunny, I have to help out in the house; that makes me sad. I love summer because she's outside more often then. She sits on her padded chair and reads, not that shopping stuff, proper books. Sometimes, she stretches out on her lounger and falls asleep letting the sun play along her skin until the shadows cover her. She always uses a high-factor lotion; factor fifty it says, and it's usually from Boots, it makes her gleam and look slippery, like an elegant fish. She rubs the lotion along her arms, her legs, the back of her neck, under her straps. I could do that.

    When she buys new clothes, and she does this regularly, she always tries them on as soon as she's home. She'll bounce up her stairs, two at a time probably, tossing her coat onto the banister, desperate to see what she looks like in that full-length mirror.

Lost and Found

She'd never shop at some discount store or anywhere like that; her bags come from the high-end chains. And she buys such a lot, dresses, trousers, jackets, cardigans, skirts, lingerie. Most of the time she draws the curtains, but sometimes she forgets, not thinking anyone would ever notice.

She's quite vain, always tweaking and brushing, smiling at her reflection, playing with her hair. As I said, summer's my favourite, no more dressing gowns and pyjamas. She likes standing in her window, the painted nails caressing her flesh. When the light's perfect, there's nothing hidden but she doesn't seem bothered.

She keeps her windows open when it's warm, too. I hear her. And him. I have to close mine. I don't want to hear him grunting like the pig he must be. He's quite different from what I expected. I always thought she'd prefer a professional, you know, a manager, lawyer or perhaps even a doctor. Someone with a decent suit and tidy hair, the type of man who drives a BMW 3 series, plays squash to keep himself in shape. A fine wine, foreign cinema and cricket man, not like him. He looks like he's dressed himself under a hedge, and he never looks clean, though I'm sure he must be. He's never clean-shaven either. That stubble must scratch her face.

She sings when she hangs his things out. He wears check shorts under those tatty blue trousers he seems to live in. She pats them as she pegs them up, rubbing them against her cheek, feeling his flesh again. Smiling. Those shorts disgust me, especially when the wind blows them into the tiny transparent panties that appear when he's there. When he's gone, it's all cotton shorts. Sometimes, they match the large moulded cups she can't possibly fill. I'm happier when he isn't there. That's when her light's on all night. I hope she's just reading.

I hate it when he talks to her from upstairs and you can easily tell what he isn't wearing. Some of the things he says shock even me, but she doesn't seem to mind. I suppose he does work, though he's too unkempt to be a professional. He cut that bird's-nest once. Everyone heard her.

"What've you done that for? You know how I love it long."

"It was getting in the way."

"But why all of it?"

"It was easier. Don't worry, it'll grow. It'll grow."

He's always able to pacify her. I was glad the windows were shut then, even more glad when he snapped the curtains to, because he was already half naked. Like a new egg.

My heart cracked when I first saw the sign poking from the front lawn. It had to be his doing, she wouldn't choose to leave. She was standing in her doorway, talking to the workmen. I hadn't noticed she'd had its dusty-red repainted. She had those jeans on, the boyfriend-style she likes, a band T-shirt, and her toes painted scarlet, as usual.

"Think it'll sell quickly?"

"Shouldn't have too much trouble with this one, love," one of the men leered. How dare he call her his love? He doesn't know her. "Great for a couple, this. You been here long?"

"Few years."

"You staying local?"

"No, off to the sunshine."

"Really? Big change then? Can't blame you. I'd love to live in the sun, but the wife won't have it. Kids settled and all that. Good for you girl. New life, eh?"

"Oh definitely a new life. Can't be any worse than this one. It's a nice area though. Quiet. No one bothers you. I like that."

"Can't really ask for more can you?"

My breath clawed at my throat. All I wanted to do was flee. I hated him so much. This was his fault. He's making her leave. I thought his accent was out of place.

All I could do was log on and locate the details, just to be inside with her, again. They always take pictures, it quickens the sale. I know how many bedrooms she has, how large her lounge is, how her attic's converted for storage and how her garage is accessed through the kitchen. What I didn't know fully were the contents of that bedroom; the carved bed with the familiar white linen, the artistic prints and an overlarge black and white photograph of a bespectacled man dominating one wall. The fairy lights were something of a surprise. She'd draped them above her bed, the bed I know he's slept in, with her. He must leave things in that chest of drawers, or the wardrobe. His checked boxer shorts, scruffy polo shirts and baggy pants contaminating hers. The furniture's co-ordinating, of course, and everything's immaculate. She must have spent hours sorting because she isn't always the tidiest; her windows weren't washed for nearly three years. The carpet's red throughout; one room's used as a sort of office study space, complete with trendy notebook computer and a wall of books. The bathroom's unexpectedly small: I'm not sure how even she fits into that bath, perhaps that's why she prefers a shower. She stands under the gush, first washing her hair, then works downwards.

The lounge is stylish, of course. Two sofas in a subdued sage look accommodating. One's a three-seater, that's probably the one he swings his legs onto to watch her flat-screened TV, hanging from the wall, or listen to her music on the Bose iPod dock. Books line the walls, along with DVDs, CDs, the trappings of someone like her. It's a home anyone would love. I'd sit neatly on her sofa, he probably just sprawls open-legged, leaving his shoes on when he first walks in. I'd never do that.

Her kitchen's quite plain; light-coloured units, photos and magnets on the fridge, a microwave and built-in hob and oven. He's the only one who uses it. He fancies himself a chef, chopping, dicing, slicing, stirring, tasting. The smells are always more exotic when he's there and I hope he chokes on it.

The price seems very reasonable, I'd pay more. Perhaps she doesn't need the money, wherever she's going. I take the virtual tour, feeling her presence in all the images. No one else should live there. I don't want to think of anyone else standing in front of her smeary windows. Then suddenly it's easy. I know exactly what I must do, the site's telling me. I can do it online, or by phone. But something holds me a moment. Perhaps I'll just read the details again, retrace the images, spend a little more time just thinking, about her, alone in her house.

There, I know what to do now. Click on the hyperlink, that's it. All I need do is wait for the response. Anyone can do it. It's simple. Takes minutes. The agent replies. He's called Jeff, and he arranges it all. He asks me when would be convenient, gives me the times she's suggested as best for her. I tell him my choice, he promises to mail me straight away or would I prefer a call?

"No, email's fine, thank you." I don't trust my voice enough to share an actual conversation.

"Give me ten minutes he says."

That's all it takes.

A VIEW TO A KILL

Don Nixon

Dinner was over. He finished his coffee and looked across at her. She rummaged in her bag and spread out the brochures from the agency. For a moment he indulged in the fantasy scenario that had obsessed him since they had come to the hotel on the border of the dark forest that might have been a setting for a tale by the Brothers Grimm. A drive into its depths on a night like this, a sudden blow to the back of the head and a speedy burial in a remote shallow grave. He thought of the spade he kept in the boot of his car and smiled as he visualised the scene. But could he do it? Would he have the nerve?

"Are you listening, George?"

His wife's shrill voice jerked him back to reality. She pushed the estate agent's folder over to him. "I've marked the ones I visited today while you were wasting your time and my money with that golf pro. Now it's your turn."

She pointed to the glossy photograph of a small eighteenth-century country house. "It's a real possibility if they come down on the price. You can view tomorrow. The agent tells me the family's bankrupt. Only the widow left. We could make a killing here."

Lost and Found

He checked a sigh. When his wife had scooped a fortune on the lottery, he would have been happy to stay in their modern bungalow but Edith wanted a big house with servants. Now they were travelling throughout the country looking for a property that matched her requirements. She had brushed aside his mild protests, her voice rising in that metallic whine that he had come to loathe.

"You're such a little man, George. So limited in your horizons. Can't you see that this is my chance to be somebody? Somebody that people will look up to and respect. When has anyone ever respected you?"

George smiled and sipped his coffee and thought of a shallow grave in the forest. The agent had been double booked so the owner showed him round. She had been waiting for him on the steps leading up to the ornate entrance under the portico.

"Diana Alleyn." Her voice had that high cutting edge forged in a top girls' public school. He was suddenly nervous. If he had been wearing a cap he would have touched it. Portraits lined the sweeping staircase.

"Are these in the asking price?" he ventured.

"'Fraid not. Need all the loot I can get. The death duties are steep. All go to auction except her." She pointed to the picture of a striking young woman dressed in the costume of a Greek nymph. "Can't let that one go. She's my favourite. They say I have her eyes. She ran off to Italy with her music master and then nearly bagged Nelson in Naples before the

Hamilton woman got her claws into him. She knew what she wanted and took it. I admire that."

He looked again at the portrait. He found he desperately wanted to impress this attractive woman. "With those clouds it might be a Constable," he said diffidently.

For the first time Diana looked closely at this little man. He was gauche and the accent was pure Estuary but with a new haircut and a good tailor he could be quite presentable. He blushed at her stare of frank appraisal. She shook her head.

"Only a copy I'm afraid. The original went long ago." She smiled at him more warmly. The agent had mentioned loads of money but wasn't there a wife? She touched his arm approvingly. "But how clever of you to recognise the style. You're the only person I've met who has spotted it."

He blushed. Was he being teased? He realised he didn't care. For the first time he felt at ease alone with a good-looking woman.

"Don't move," she commanded. "If you're going to buy this place then I'd better let you into the family secret that's not in the agent's brochure."

She motioned him to follow her up the staircase and pressed a wooden rosette in the wall panelling. The step in front of him suddenly fell away. He flinched and clutched the bannister rail. She laughed and pressed the rosette again and the stair returned to its original position.

"Nasty, isn't it? That's the doing of the first Viscount in 1780. He literally got away with murder." She sat down on the top step and lit a cigarette. "He'd run through his wife's dowry and was desperate for money so he had the stairs made. They found her one morning at the foot of this staircase with a broken neck. Very Amy Robsart. He married another heiress. The secret was kept in the family. I'm the only one left who knows."

"But you've told me."

She held his gaze and her fingers played with the gold chain at her throat. "Yes, I've told you. Of course we could just keep it a secret between the two of us. It might put some people off." She held out her hand and he helped her rise. "Do think your wife will like the house?"

He paused and she withdrew her hand. He gingerly tapped a foot on the treacherous stair. "With your help she might just fall for it," he said slowly.

***

To George's surprise, Edith did not argue over the asking price and got on well with Diana. "I like her," she said. "She's not a snob and she'll be useful for introductions."

He found that most days she was with Diana planning the move. She refused his offers to drive her to the house. "You would be bored stiff, George. Lot of girls' talk. New curtains and carpets. Planning dinner parties. All girlie stuff. You keep on with your golf lessons."

On the rare occasions he managed to see Diana alone, he told her of the transforming effect she was having on his wife. "Not that her good mood will last," he said. He suddenly realised how jealous he was of his wife's monopolising of Diana.

A few days before the contract was due to be signed, Diana invited them to dinner. "It will be a very simple affair I'm afraid. No servants live in any more so we'll have to serve ourselves."

After dinner, Edith marched upstairs to the drawing room. George was embarrassed. His wife was already assuming the hostess role. He glanced at Diana. She gave a little shrug. "Oh! I forgot. The coffee is in flasks in the pantry downstairs. We should have brought it up with us."

"George can get it." Edith motioned him away.

"The tray is ready," said Diana. "And George don't forget to bring that special molasses sugar I got for Edith to try for her diabetes. It's in the red Murano dish. The one I told you the first Viscount brought back from Italy for his first wife. Now that Edith likes the house, perhaps we ought to introduce her to the first Viscount. After all, women always fall for him."

George felt a surge of excitement. He heard them laughing as he began to climb the staircase. The tray was heavy. Diana was waiting at the top. He saw her reach for the wooden rosette. She hesitated. Edith appeared behind her.

"Do it," she hissed. "Do it now."

Diana pressed the rosette. As he fell backwards, he saw his wife's triumphant face.

Edith looked down at the still body of her husband. She patted Diana's arm approvingly. "Such a silly little man," she murmured. She frowned as she saw the shattered pieces of Murano glass, scattered like bloodstains on the stairs. "Pity the bowl had to go as well." She turned to Diana. "Just add it to the sum we agreed."

Diana nodded. Edith saw with amusement that her companion's face was white. So much for aristocratic sang-froid she thought contemptuously. She had wondered when they were planning the murder if Diana might be a problem. If so, she would have to deal with her, but not yet. They would need to get through the next few days together when the questions started. She looked down again at the crumpled body of her husband and visualised Diana lying there in his place. It would certainly leave everything tidy. But that was for the future.

"Get the car," she ordered. "The spade and tarpaulin's in the back. We should be in the forest in ten minutes. I know just the place. I've followed George there a few times when he was pretending to go to the golf course. He chose a very quiet spot and he hasn't left much digging to do."

She smiled. "Always so helpful, George."

POSTCARD FROM DELANOS, WICHITA

Lynne Voyce

When the first fist-sized hailstones hit my sultry skin, as I rush along West Douglas Avenue towards Dollar General, it is welcome relief – ice cubes from heaven. They distract me, just as the rattle of them on the windscreen distracts the driver. By the time I realise that the blue station wagon is hurtling towards me there is nothing I can do. I have stepped off the kerb and am in midair.

I see the driver's face in forensic detail: the glint of sugar on his lips from the doughnut in his hand, the indent across his forehead where his work hat has sat all day, the weary, home-bound look in his eyes. I wanted to get home too, kick off my shoes, pull a Pepsi from the fridge, be alone. It has been so hot in the bank, all day; thirty-six degrees the manager's thermometer had said. The air conditioning was broken but he wouldn't let us go home. Instead he gave us water and propped the doors open. It gets so hot in Kansas in the summer. Landlocked, you see. Right in the middle of this great big, beautiful continent.

Then the station wagon hits. The impact takes my legs from under me and I do a gymnastic twist in the air. First, I see the steel blue paint of the chassis; then a drab expanse of sky; then the wide grey tarmac of Douglas Avenue, the shallow precipice of the kerb cutting through it. But when I turn again I am not met by the grille of the station wagon. Instead, the line of the pavement has melted into a jagged cliff edge. On one side is clipped, emerald grass, on the other a sheer drop. At the bottom, on the muted, wet shingle, is a body, naked, half way between man and boy, face down and dead on the beach. It is the body I saw thirty years ago. When I'd first discovered it I'd screamed and screamed, ran into the house (such a long way in those days), to tell my mother. When we returned it was gone, reclaimed by the sea to be washed up again the next day on the sands at Weymouth. This time, instead of fleeing, I swoop down to see him close up. There is seaweed over his head and neck, gleaming sapphire tendrils entwined in his hair, and through the spread of its fingers I see a tiny navy blue heart inked on the blade of his shoulder. The curve of his back and the rise of his buttocks make him seem part of the landscape, not something flat and dead. The soles of his feet, facing the sky, are soft and pale, belying a lifetime of walking on sand.

  Then I turn to the cliff, will myself to move up its alternate grey and terracotta strata, testament to its ancient history and constant metamorphosis. At the top I am met with a vision of my father revving the small petrol engine of his lawnmower, ready to cut the ever-decreasing lawn. He is as old as he should be. This isn't a childhood memory. When I look towards

Postcard from Delanos, Wichita

the tall red brick house I see the white crown of mother's permed hair, protruding above the back of the armchair. Such a shame everything faces away from the view; their way of denying the sea is coming ever closer. I wonder if the effort of doing her hair keeps a few more fragments of past in her head. I have always intended to go back but she wouldn't know me anymore. And to fly the Atlantic is a risk. I took that risk once to get to Delanos, Wichita.

Father pushes the mower towards the cliff. I can see that the pansies and marigolds he planted on the farthest beds are now lying in the mud and rubble at the bottom of the drop. Soon, when the tide is high, their pretty gold and purple petals will be dragged into the insistent sea, pulled to its depths with the undercurrents, just as the body of the youth was. Still, my father smiles as he acknowledges the few brave flowers, clinging to the land, glistening in the weak, morning sun.

"The council will find us a bungalow in town," he had said on the phone yesterday. "Your mother said it would be over her dead body, that she'd rather tumble into the sea and be damned. She said it right to me though. She knew who she was talking to." The crackle in his voice became the crackle on the long-distance line. "We'd love to see you Faren, before ..." I remained silent. I wanted to stay safe, right in the middle, right in Kansas.

When I was a child, Dad would take his sandwich box and ride his bike to work. And each time my mother would say, just as she said to me when I left for school, "Don't go close to the edge," in reference to the ever-present, advancing cliffs. It became synonymous with "goodbye."

"Don't go close to the edge," I mouth to him now but he doesn't hear or see me.

The next moment I am facing my mother. She is an empty, flickering bulb of a woman. Then slowly, in front of me, like a time-lapse film running backwards, the years fall away. Once again she is the woman from my childhood: her hair is the iridescent black of a starling's wing; her face is ripe and youthful; her blank stare is now an all-seeing gaze, transmitting that familiar sense of rising panic. Then she is no longer on the armchair but sitting on the candlewick quilt of my bed as I look up at her.

"It was just a nightmare, Faren," she is saying, smoothing my hair against my skull. I remember that the nightmare was – is – always about the young man. "He was a reckless boy from a reckless family – remember that: his father is a travelling magician, that must tell you something, and his mother sings the clubs," she continues, her kohl-rimmed eyes wide, her frosted lips pursed. "You're not like that. We're not like that. He had been diving off the head of rocks in the dark, drunk with his friends. Accidents like that only happen to the reckless, dear. Still, you must never forget to be careful because the sea took him and it will take you if you fall."

Postcard from Delanos, Wichita

As the edge crept ever closer, year on year, tearing strips off the garden, the warning became more emphatic: "Don't go close to the edge," every time I left the house. In fact we never said "goodbye," or "have a good day," or even "I love you" before any one of us left. We'd always say: "Don't go close to the edge." I even said it too, after a while. Of course the edge was much further away then than it is now as my mother transforms back into a desolate husk and I watch my dad through the living-room window, mowing the lawn. That is what is so pitiful about it all. Eventually we knew that we would all be close to the edge, or even over it: dad, mum, me, the house, the shed, the marigolds and pansies.

I have spent my life trying to avoid it. When eventually I left home I went as far away from the coast as I could, right into the heart of the industrial Midlands. But still I felt the brink of our island creeping closer. I'd lie in the middle of my bed at night and feel the rim of my mattress with my fingers; it might as well have been the edge of the land. So, soon I felt the pull of the big, safe continent across the Atlantic. There was nothing spontaneous about the move. It wasn't an adventure. I secured a bank job and a ground floor flat, and that was that. And twenty years later I am crossing West Douglas Avenue, going to get cotton from Dollar General, to hem the curtains in my little flat where I live alone. But today I stepped off the kerb a moment too late.

Lost and Found

Dad moves back and forth on the foreshortened lawn, like a sleepwalker: from the fence by the lane to the edge and back again, over and over. He looks out. Perhaps he is thinking of me. The sea is choppy and restless. Then, in a momentary lapse of concentration, he lets go of the lawnmower. When he blinks back to attention, it is gone, powering with its revving petrol engine toward the threshold. Then finally, as it launches itself into the seamless blue grey of sea and sky, the driver of the station wagon drops the last morsel of his doughnut into his lap and I hit the tarmac.

DANGEROUS TUESDAY

Angela Williams

By the time the 8.22 am arrived at Epping station it was nearly always full, standing room only. In those days, on hot summer mornings, the double doors of the Sydney commuter trains were left open for the journey into the city. If you fell out, it was your neck, but nobody ever did. Jim, Warren and Shorty gathered on the same platform every day to travel in together for their first real day jobs after school, conspicuous by their brand new, cheap white shirts, big collars and stiff, shiny shoes. It was a matter of competitive pride among them to avoid the stuffy still air inside the carriage, waiting till the last possible minute on the platform and then running like hell to jump on. They hung from the poles by the doors for the hour into the city, shouting and joking over the rattle of the wheels and the rush of cool wind.

On that morning, she was quick and lithe among the grey commuters, a cotton bag slung over her brown bare shoulders. As the train rolled away from the platform, she leapt lightly onto the moving carriage, ducking into the gap beside Jim.

He was not the only one to notice her. The campaign began almost immediately. Warren, who already had his own car, delivered his devastating opener.

Lost and Found

"Hi bewdyful, can I take your picture? I want to show Santa just what I want this Christmas."

A chorus of snorts and loud guffaws from the other two sabotaged his opening advantage. The girl grinned and ignored them. She stood so close to Jim, her long hair brushing his cheek in the breeze from the open doors, that he could not speak.

Each fresh morning the carriages bowled under the arching girders of the Harbour Bridge. From the open door they could see the whole of the harbour spread out below them. Morning sunlight flashed in rapid semaphore off the apartment windows that crowded down the steep shores to the water's edge. Great tankers and liners, oblivious to the chaos of the tiny ferries hurrying around them, ploughed their way out to the Heads, the ocean and the world beyond. On the far side of the bridge, their train was swallowed underground into the dark mouth of the city and all the banter dried up with the thought of the day ahead in fluorescent-lit offices.

A pay cheque each month made the commute bearable but the money never lasted long so most weekends the boys had to resort to drinking cheap beer at Shorty's mum's place. They sat on the concrete steps facing onto the dusty backyard, cracking open cans and putting the world to rights. On such evenings, the girl on the train became the subject of much discussion. They called her Tuesday, because none of them was brave enough to ask the direct question. Shorty thought maybe she was a model and he was nominated to find out but even under his clumsy, harmless charm she remained elusive.

There were plenty of other girls around, feral blondes who prowled the Epping Hotel bar in packs, and got wasted on rum and Cokes. Despite Warren's best efforts, Jim had strenuously avoided them all. Yet this slender girl, who stepped in beside him every Tuesday, was making his nights restless.

So when he caught sight of her, swinging her way easily through the city lunchtime crowds down George Street, he had to follow her. He tracked her, glimpsed at a distance down the broad avenue, half running to keep up with her, through the chains of traffic lights and queuing cars. On she went, past the slick boutiques then downtown past the Chinese restaurants, trussed crispy ducks roasting in the windows – now into deep canyons of shabby rag trade warehouses where sewing machines could be heard clattering above.

At last he thought he saw her disappear through a metal door of one of the buildings, and he stood confused and breathless. If he went in it would be obvious he had chased her all that way. Girls were a foreign country to him and this girl was the first. He dared not get it wrong but he had no idea how to get it right.

Above him from the open warehouse window, a piano played, a lilt and turn to the notes distracting him so that he did not notice her standing beside him, laughing at his shock.

Lost and Found

"Hey Jim, what took you so long? Come on." She linked cool long fingers through his and led him inside.

At the far end of a long room, a group of skinny girls stood poised on one leg. In one movement, alert and flighty as a flock of pink flamingos, they swivelled their heads to stare expectantly at him. Tuesday dropped her bag to the wooden floor, wound her hair into a tight knot and began unceremoniously to strip layers off in front of him whilst he, blushing, backed away and the flamingos cackled.

At the first note of the piano, their attention was instantly diverted and the flock swirled, parted and dived, oblivious to his presence. He sat on an old plastic chair by the wall watching her dance, so close he could see the light catch the sheen of sweat on the arc of her back.

The train gang kept a respectful distance from the pair of them for the rest of the summer on the morning commute. Warren denounced her as "a dangerous chick" and stated pointedly that only pseudos went to the ballet, but he was still pretty dirty about being rejected by her so nobody took any notice. In any case, it was too embarrassing to watch Jim lose all his dignity as they leaned cocooned together at the back of the carriage.

He blew all his savings and bought a car, just to be alone with her; a beat up Holden panel wagon, which he washed scrupulously or the boys would leave lewd messages in the dust on the paintwork.

Sometimes, when she could get away, they drove out through the baking suburbs to Bilgolah Beach, parked under the Norfolk pines and swam together after sunset in the velvet black surf. As they made love in the back of the van, the soft ocean breeze cooling their skin through the open doors, Jim knew this was it. Nothing else seemed possible or better.

By autumn that year the sweltering city glowered. Hot, dusty southerly winds gave no relief, and the earth plummeted out of his perfect universe. It was Tuesday morning and Jim stood alone in the sweaty crowded carriage, his back turned to the boys. Only Shorty dared to speak to him.

"You been dumped?"

"You catch on quick."

"Keep your hair on. Just asking."

"She had to go to London, she won a scholarship."

"You not going then?"

"Yeah right. As if. I wasn't ever part of the plan. That's what her mum said anyway."

Shorty looked closely at him. "Dude, you're worth ten of her," he said, and turned away abruptly.

Jim hung his head outside the open train doors. The rush of air filled his open mouth, his cheeks distorting to a puffy grimace, tears blasting back horizontally into his ears. Ahead, beneath the grey mess of cables and girders flickering past, he could see the northbound train barrelling toward him on the narrow parallel track. He leaned out, casually, one hand grasping the safety rail above his head, one foot on the lip of the doorway, until his body dangled star-like over the rushing void, his hair plastered flat and shirt ballooning behind. A long, discordant warning blast sounded from the oncoming train. Two more blasts, louder, sharper and urgent. Still he hung out, daring it closer to the last second, wanting the surge of adrenaline to obliterate the tight ache in his chest, and still the rust red sheer wall of the oncoming train slid inexorably towards him, the locked steel wheels screeching and sparking. He could see the face of the driver through the oily screen glass; the shadow of the great engine engulfed him; and he knew with paralysed clarity that this time he had left it too late.

Just over a year afterwards, Warren and Shorty saw the girl for the last time. She was standing waiting on the platform at Epping on a Tuesday morning, her hair cropped, a slight, tired figure, balancing a baby on one hip. Shorty recognised her, stepped forward and spoke quietly with her. She listened, face upturned to his, shrank from his outstretched hand and turned and made her way slowly back up the stairs, holding the baby tight against the tide of grey suited morning commuters pouring onto the station, buffeting and flowing around her.

    These days the line from Epping station carries fast quiet double decker trains, air conditioned with windows and doors automatically sealed shut. Above the Harbour Bridge, tourists crawl like chains of ants up its high shoulders, securely strapped and clipped to the girders. All risks have been assessed and accidents hardly ever happen.

THE SHADOW

Laura Harrhy

On Christmas Day I put Charlotte in a coma. My intentions had been good, of course: on payday I put a tightly rolled quartet of £20 notes into a plastic film canister, hidden in the toe of one of my foulest smelling trainers, leaving me with a reduced budget of £20 for her Christmas gift, but a step closer to the engagement ring I planned to propose with. Naturally, I know nothing about hair straighteners, but as I wrapped the £6.99 pair I picked up at the market I naively felt I was marching towards glory.

The day came, as it does but once a year, and her excited eyes reflected flashes of tinsel as she tore open the paper I had laboriously handmade over a bucket of slurried newspaper and rose petals. It became possibly the most romantic kindling in history as her gift overheated and sparked. Presumably the next thing to catch was the tree. I was changing out of my pyjamas and into my Sunday best; she was putting the turkey in the oven as she waited for the straighteners to heat up, but when I ran out of the bedroom, smoke had already filled her delicate pink lungs. I didn't think to check her pulse; instead I snatched her up off the tiled floor and into my arms, shouldered open the door to the balcony, and after pausing a moment to look at the blush still present in her cheeks, dropped

The Shadow

her horizontally over the railing into the snow fifteen feet below.

In a stressful situation, the mind becomes sieve-like, but the gist of what the consultant had to say was that he was unsure if it was the smoke or the fall that actually rendered her comatose, however in either case, I had undoubtedly saved her life. He had seemingly been trained in the art of not mentioning that the events of the day were nevertheless my fault; but I morbidly brooded on the paradox each time I stood at the foot of her bed, my eyes slackening their focus on reality and peering into the middle distance.

I continued to save £20 notes and ironically managed to save for the ring faster now that I only had myself to buy for, and no cinema outings or evenings in restaurants to finance. I knelt on the easy chair next to her bed and took her hand, stroking the soft skin, before slipping the ring into place and kissing her forehead. As I walked home, I stopped at a park and threw pebbles into the lake. I imagined Charlotte as a child, dreaming of her engagement. I supposed she had hoped to be conscious for it. She must have imagined her wedding day, her dress, and the cake, maybe setting up her dolls to act it out. I didn't know: I met her at work at the age of twenty-seven. No dolls were present.

I continued my walk home, daydreaming of scenes from her youth, wishing we could have grown up together and shared our school days and adolescence. What is it they say? – be careful what you wish for; speak of the Devil, and all that.

***

The agent met me at reception, and invited me to follow her deeper into the clinic. She was blonde; smiling; wearing too much make-up. She reminded me of a dental nurse. I had been expecting a set-up involving a virtual reality helmet, but the anteroom she led me into was small and tiled. A slight smile flickered across my face as I imagined the white overall attired girl hosing the blood of the previous customer off the walls, but surprise overcame me as she turned a dimmer switch and soft lighting grew: the small chamber led into a large, luxurious bathroom, furnished in a feminine manner with orchids, pot pourri, and scented candles, which were already burning. The tiles were a modern, glittered marble, and a pile of soft towels begged the visitor to remove their clothes. The blonde crossed to a large circular bathtub, sunken into the centre of the floor, and equipped with a silver safety strap that fitted across the chest of the participant. She opened the taps and a viscous, golden liquid with the appearance of thick oil, but the scent of lavender, spilled out. Next, she selected a fat-bottomed teardrop of a jar from a shelf arranged by colour and poured a generous measure under the running tap. I hadn't thought that oil could foam, but clouds of gentle, lilac bubbles began to grow on the surface. At last she turned to me and smiled. I was first to speak.

"So … is this a time machine?"

"No."

"Is this a travel machine?"

"No."

"Is it magic?"

"No."

"Is it drugs?"

"No."

"Not a hallucination then?"

"No."

"Hypnosis?"

"No."

I ran out of questions, and I thought she was going to say "No" again, out of habit, but she smiled.

"It is an … experience. A shadow of the past, bending as light through a prism in order to incorporate you." She held out a hand, presumably for my clothes. My eyes swivelled down in my head to follow her movement, which must have given me a reluctant air. She smiled again, more stiffly, in the manner of one trying to remain patient in the face of the difficult behaviour of a small nephew whose parents are present.

"Your desire in visiting our clinic was to spend a day with your girlfriend, at a point in her past before she met you. Our only rules are, you must not tell her how you came to be there, and the visit must remain entirely platonic. You also need to get into that bath."

Lost and Found

***

Butterflies and dragonflies danced across my field of vision. This was not my usual bath-time experience, and I tried to raise an eyebrow, but it is not easy to be sardonic while unconscious. Unconscious? I hadn't noticed. The lilac goo filling the bath was sneakier than the anaesthetist at hospital. He had at least asked me to count backwards from ten the day I was surgically removed from my appendix. I was just in the middle of hoping that I wouldn't drown in hot gloop, when it dawned on me that I was walking through a meadow, dressed in shorts. My legs were skinnier than I remembered, and less hairy. Presently, I came across a chestnut-haired girl playing on a swing. She smiled at me as I approached, and the gap in her teeth dated her to around the age of eight.

I seemed to be looking at her through the sparkling water of a snow globe, and hearing her through a tin-can phone system, but we spent a happy few hours together, playing on the swings and talking. Although I seemingly had the body of a kid of a similar age to her, I had kept my own mind, and as she talked of ponies and fairies I was enchanted: this was my Charlotte, only different, talking to me like to a brother about the insignificant minutiae that made her happy. I wanted to listen forever.

After this, I returned to the clinic every day after work, filling my credit card with the price of these happy moments. Each time we met, Charlotte seemed to remember me, and I began to spend longer and longer in the "experience". I suppose I was falling in love with her again, but it began to take its toll. Initially I had simply wanted to know her more fully, ready for when she woke. But as time passed I began to visit the real-life Sleeping Beauty that was the Charlotte of the present day less and less, and I grew thin as I spent my money and time on the experiences rather than on food. The women at the clinic were curious about my repeated, lengthy visits, and they tried to discourage the high frequency of my appointments, but I tipped them enough to keep them courteous and acquiescent.

When Charlotte died, thirteen months after the fire, her parents let me bury her wearing the diamond ring I had bought. Immediately after the funeral, I went to the clinic. I slid into the goo and when the smiling blonde woman closed the door behind her, I unbuckled the safety strap, resolving that, during my slumber, fate would decide if I should slip deeper into the warm liquid.

I found Charlotte, aged fifteen or so, sitting cross-legged in her parents' garden, weaving a crown and bracelet from a selection of flowers and petals strewn on the grass around her. I sat down next to her and handed her a rose and she looked up at me and smiled. Her hair fell in soft brown waves to her shoulders, never having met a straightening iron, unblemished and perfect.

MR MYSTERY'S LION

Clare Kirwan

"You are a lion," Mr Mystery told her, his moustache twitching. "Ferocious! Yes? Animal Magic! Yes? Grrrr!"

Abigail nodded weakly; the sleeves of the beige velvet costume were too long and it was saggy at the knees. But Mr Mystery had said it was too late to fix that now, what with the show starting in half an hour. There was still a wet stain down the front where Lucy's sick had been mopped up, but once the head was on nobody would notice, he said.

Lucy had resisted being replaced, of course.

"But the show must go on!" she had protested. Lucy was older, nearly twelve. She was always saying how important it was to be professional. "What would Bonnie Langford do?" she always asked. Or: "Do you think we'll get onto *New Faces* looking miserable like that?"

"The show will go on," Mr Mystery replied. "Abigail knows what to do – she's seen you do it often enough and she's got to start some time."

He had helped Lucy out of the costume and she stomped away. Abigail – who was usually the magic rabbit – felt guilty and excited and scared, all mixed up together. She wished her mum was there, but Mum didn't come to the shows when they were out of town.

Mr Mystery's Lion

Mr Mystery lived just across town in one of the big old houses. He had shown Abigail the basement once, where he made all his illusions. It smelled of sawdust and varnish and was full of marvellous things. Mr Mystery said that she could visit any time, but that it was a secret place. Abigail knew by now that you have to keep a lot of secrets in magic – it was part of the code.

"It's a wonder how he's brought that girl out of her shell!" Mum was proud of telling the neighbours. "He's so good with the young ones."

"You have to think like a lion, move like a lion. Remember how I taught you? Grrr! Grrr!" Mr Mystery had chased her around backstage, then he made her chase him. But even though she tried not to go too fast, he had let her catch him. He liked to play funny games but he only spoke with a funny accent during the show, the rest of the time he spoke the same as everyone else.

"Five minutes," said the spotty young man who was doing the lights.

"Places everyone!" shouted My Mystery. Abigail climbed into the wooden box that was painted like a dog house, squeezing into the secret compartment above the thick black curtain. Then Bouncer was bundled into the front space behind the diagonal mirror – she could hear him scrabbling and snuffling around beneath her.

"Good boy," she whispered. "It's okay. It's going to be okay."

She wasn't sure the dog could understand, but she liked hearing her own words squished there in the dark with her.

Their intro music started up on the cassette player – a rousing blast of brass that made her toes tingle every time she heard it. She could only see a tiny thread of the light where the top panels met. The sound of the music and the audience rustling still made her feel giddy even from inside the box, and the smell of Lucy's sick mingled with Bouncer's doggy breath in the enclosed space made her gag. But the show must go on. Abigail breathed deeply and concentrated: "I am a lion. I am ferocious and beautiful, and I prowl in the heart of the African ..." She was going to say "jungle", but instead a picture came into her head of bright plains with tall grass and orange earth, a brilliant blue sky.

Outside, Mr Mystery spun the dog house around and flung the door open, revealing the empty space. Then he shut the door and spun it round a few more times, leaving it facing the opposite way.

"I am a lion, in the deep long grass, under the burning sun. I am strong."

She didn't feel strong. Mr Mystery always won the play fights. And she didn't feel strong when he levitated her – she tried really hard to make herself feel extra light so she wouldn't come crashing to the floor, holding her breath as he passed the hoop over and around her, trying not to flinch if he touched her.

Mr Mystery's Lion

He was standing nearby now, talking in his funny voice: "Can you tell me what iz in zee box?"

"Oh yes, Mr Mystery!" said the new girl.

But she'd got the line wrong – that was a line from later on. You always had to say the line right or it would be worse later. Mr Mystery was very strict about that. The new girl had looked even funnier in the monkey costume than Maisie used to. Maisie's dad wouldn't let her come any more. She hadn't even said goodbye.

"I *said*: Can you tell me what iz in zee box?" Abigail knew he would be smiling, flashing his enormous white teeth. But his voice wasn't smiling.

"It's empty!" The girl squeaked.

"Ye-es. Silly monkey! We all saw zat it was empty, didn't we?"

There was a sharp crack of sound – his wand being struck on the painted wood. That sound always made Abigail jump but she heard the younger girl gasp somewhere near the box. She was a nervous little thing. Abigail decided she would make friends with her, whatever Lucy said.

"But look!"

Bouncer's claws scrabbled on the wood as the front door opened and he scampered out of the box. The poor creature was always dazed at this point – with the spotlights suddenly in his eyes and the audience clapping. Abigail hoped the new girl would look after him nicely. It was important to take care of your animals, give them attention, show them who is in charge. Mr Mystery had taught her that.

"I am a lion," she told herself. "I can roar and run faster than anything. I am powerful and I can kill a man." Her limbs were stiff from crouching. Lucy was bigger than her – how did she even fit inside? "I am a lion, crouching in the undergrowth, waiting to leap ..."

She was hot. The smell of sick was overpowering, and the smell of Bouncer too, with the staleness of the box and the sharp tang of the polish they used on the stage. Worst of all, the scent of Mr Mystery's cologne close by as he opened the front door one more time to show how the dog house really was empty this time. She hated that smell.

"And what iz in zee box now, everybody?"

"It's empty!" A few voices replied.

"I can't hear you," Mr Mystery made his voice sound scary sometimes. It made the little children giggle with fear, the ones who didn't know him.

"It's empty!" The low growl of more voices.

Mr Mystery spun the box round and round, deftly releasing the top catch ready for the finale. Abigail held on, bracing herself against the side, tense and dizzy. She wasn't sure which way she was facing any more, where she was.

"I'm a lion," she told herself, over and over, pressing her eyes shut and willing it so. "Abracadabra! I'm a lion."

The air stirred in the dark, bringing other scents she didn't recognise.

There was a sharp crack on the roof – her signal to jump out of the top. "Ta da!" Mr Mystery would say. She tensed her leg muscles and sprang ...

... out into a wide, bright savannah with hot dust in her nostrils and the scent of young animals beginning to sense danger.

WATCHING

Valerie West

You have to understand I did not wish to hurt anyone; that was never my intention. I acknowledge that my inclinations are not conventional, but I did all I could not to let them impinge on my professional life. No doubt you will point out that it was a mistake to take up teaching and, on reflection, I would have to agree with you, but at the age of twenty I was very idealistic about being able to inspire others with my love of history; it was as simple as that. I also enjoyed the company of young people and had been involved in youth work as an undergraduate, but it was all quite innocent.

Well, perhaps I am not being quite honest with you or with myself. I was aware of a certain attraction, but initially I saw it simply as aesthetic; an admiration of the unconscious grace of young bodies. It was the pleasure of looking and nothing more. I didn't consider myself to be in any way different. After all, I made friends of both sexes while at university and I even had a girlfriend for a while although the relationship came to a natural end when we both realised that I had no intention of getting married. In retrospect, it was a great pity. She was a charming young woman and it would have benefited both of us, I think.

Watching

After a few years, I found teaching in the state system increasingly stressful. Sadly my impression was that it was more about policing than imparting knowledge, so it was with relief that I eventually obtained a post at a minor public school. It was situated in a Victorian pile on the outskirts of a small market town, apparently becalmed in the nineteen-fifties. Tweed jackets with elbow patches were de rigueur in the staff room and even at the age of thirty, I was treated very much as the young newcomer. I immediately felt at home and on my first free Saturday, I went to shop for a sports jacket.

My first form was that year's new intake and many of the boys came from service families so their parents were overseas. My youth helped to make me a natural confidant and I was touched and honoured by their trust. However it was at this time that I became more aware of … unsuitable feelings. Working with boarders gives rise to more personal contact than at an ordinary school, as you may imagine. The times which caught me off guard were the supervision of "lights out" in the dormitories and checking the changing rooms after games, but nothing inappropriate took place.

I recognised the danger and was aware of my responsibilities, so I guarded my behaviour at all times. Admittedly it could be a strain, but I loved all the other aspects of the job so much that I was determined that nothing should jeopardise it. During one summer vacation I acquired a spaniel puppy called Roland who provided companionship and gave me the excuse to take long walks. It was a useful way to take some exercise and in summer the path beside the playing fields was especially rewarding; just to observe, you understand.

Life slipped into a pleasant enough routine and although opportunities for socialising were rather limited, I usually found enough interests to fill my spare time. I founded a Local History Society and on several weekends a term, I took a group of boys on expeditions to sites of interest in the surrounding area. In retrospect, I realised that the more informal atmosphere away from school premises had led to several minor indiscretions; squeezing a shoulder in encouragement or standing a little too close to pore over a map, for instance. These meant nothing in themselves, but one day another colleague accompanied us on an expedition to a Tudor manor house in which he was particularly interested. At one point during the afternoon, I looked up from close study of a manuscript in a glass case with one of my pupils to see him giving me a hard stare and, after supper that evening, he sought me out in the Common Room.

"Look Geoffrey," he began. "You're a good form tutor and well respected. I know it's easy to get fond of these young chaps, but sometimes actions can be misconstrued. And they seem more knowing these days, somehow. Slippery slope, that's all I'm saying. Just watch your step."

Watching

I started to stammer something, but he raised a warning finger and strode off. I found a corner where I could retire behind my newspaper and hide my confusion. As you may imagine, I slept badly that night. Had I overstepped the mark? My mind was in turmoil for several weeks. I wondered whether I should resign and look for a post elsewhere, but in truth after fifteen years in that sheltered backwater, I doubted I could survive out in the real world. I resolved to be more vigilant. In reality, I hadn't *really* done anything; hardly anything at all, but it was the longing, you see. I was afraid that my palpable longing would give me away.

In the end, my downfall came from an unexpected source. A colleague from the grammar school in town contacted me to ask whether I would consider giving extra tuition to an exceptional pupil of his who wanted to try for Oxford. I agreed, but as soon as I opened my door to him, I knew that I was lost. I understand that there is something grotesque, even obscene, in the notion of a balding fifty-year-old bachelor falling in love with a sixteen-year-old boy, but that is what happened. Of course, I did not say anything to him, but his twice weekly visits became the most important thing in my life, made even more piquant because he was clearly highly intelligent and therefore a pleasure to teach. One afternoon I was elaborating on some obscure point, when I glanced up to find him regarding me with an odd smile. I felt a flicker of unease.

"Is something the matter?" I asked.

"You fancy me, don't you sir?"

I felt a sensation akin to a blow to the stomach and steadied myself against the edge of the table.

"Don't be ridiculous, young man. That is totally inappropriate. I suggest you apologise immediately."

"I don't mind, sir. It's kind of flattering … as long as you don't try anything. It's happened before, actually."

"And did they … try anything?" I couldn't look at him.

"Yeah. Our vicar, would you believe, but I managed to knee him so I got away and he couldn't say anything."

"Anyone else?"

"There's been a teacher at school who pats my arm and ruffles my hair and stuff. It's more when I catch him looking at me … like you do sir. I can tell what he's thinking."

A silence hung in the air between us in my shabby study.

"I think you'd better go," I said in a husky whisper. I cleared my throat and repeated the order.

"All right sir, if that's what you want. Same time on Thursday?"

"No, I think not. I don't think there is any more I can teach you. You should consider our sessions at an end."

He rose and gathered up his books. He headed for the door, then paused and turned to face me. "Well, thanks then, sir. It's been really useful. I'm sorry if I upset you. It's no big deal." He smiled and stuck out his hand.

I looked at it as if he was offering me a loaded gun. It took all my will power not to pull him to me; instead I shook his hand then shoved him gently away.

"Best of luck," I said and even managed a smile, but once the door closed behind him I sank into a chair and put my head in my hands.

I managed to struggle on to the end of the summer term then an unfortunate salvation offered itself in the form of my father's sudden death from a heart attack. I was able to use this as an excuse to tender my resignation so that I could move nearer to my mother and once I was settled, I bought into a partnership in a small antique shop. It is, of course, a compromise; however it still indulges my passion for history, if only obliquely.

There is a decent independent school nearby and the students regularly pass our window in their striped blazers. Roland and I still manage our daily walks and no one seems to mind an old man and his dog pausing by the playing fields to watch the cricket on a summer afternoon. It is the small pleasures that keep one going, I find.

EMERALDS

Anne-Marie Biggs

Midwinter, in the pearl-cased light of mid-afternoon, a nothing time without purpose; the dead time when the small words of lunch have faded and the comfort of evening is hours away. A heavy sky, overstuffed with snow and ready to split over the dark coats of the shoppers. Among the thin trickle at the far end of the High Street, Annette's orange jeans and scarlet jacket burned like a coal thrown from the grey embers of the clouds. She glanced at her watch and up at the sky, then crossed the road towards the flower shop. She paused outside to look at the bowls of hyacinths and was about to enter the shop when the window adjoining it caught her eye.

A rusting white birdcage trimmed with milky feather boas, books bound in dove-grey leather with faded silver lettering, ivory candlesticks and silk roses, paper-thin and glistening with diamante dewdrops. It would have looked stark and cold, except that right in the middle of the display was a glowing lantern, gold with careful latticing cut into it, studded with jewels of glass: ruby, sapphire, topaz, emerald. Annette stared at it, dazzled, and heard the whisper of a familiar voice carefully enunciating a sentence; her fingers twitched, following the curves of the sound.

Emeralds

She looked towards the florist's window again for a moment, then resolutely turned back to the antique shop and pushed at the door.

A bell sounded with a ragged clang as Annette entered. It made her jump and she almost backed out again.

"May I help you?" A woman loomed out of nowhere, holding a duster and a cramped still life.

"Um – no – yes. Well, maybe." Annette edged into the shop, uncertain now if this was a good idea after all.

"Is it something in particular you're looking for? Do come in properly before someone trips over you on the doorstep there."

Annette glanced over her shoulder, expecting to see a queue but there was no one, and the other shoppers scuttled by, heads bent against the cold, not looking.

"I'm after a present for someone I know," Annette said. "I've tried the usual shops but I haven't found anything."

A faint expression of distaste crossed the woman's face but she said nothing.

"I saw your display in the window. I thought I'd come and – have a look," Annette finished lamely.

"What sort of gift had you in mind?"

"Something a bit –"

"Different?"

"Conventional. The candlesticks in the window – I was wondering about those. How much are they?"

Candlesticks from an Egyptian trader, twenty-odd years ago; a dark market stall lit with jewelled lanterns and draped with Persian rugs; scarlet and black and threaded with gold. Candlesticks carved from ancient ivory, a craftsman's work for the Empire shivering at the wrong end of the High Street in a bland, southern town.

"I suppose they are – conventional – enough, but I have more attractive pieces." The woman reached up to a shelf and picked out two candlesticks carved from oak. "These are a little more modern in design." She flicked a glance at Annette's bright jeans and leather jacket. "Perhaps your friend would like them?"

"Perhaps. She's not a friend, really. I mean, I'm not just doing it for her, it's for someone else … Sorry." Annette stopped herself, feeling stupid. She took a breath. "I had a tutor at uni, in London, called Helen. When we were getting all in a state about the world and what was wrong with politics and all the rest of it, she used to say that everything we did made a difference, even if it was only a tiny thing. We used to call her Hippy Helen and sort of teased her but she was lovely… Anyhow, there's a secretary at work who's having a bad time and I thought I'd try and – make a difference. Even a tiny difference."

"Wouldn't flowers be more suitable?" the woman asked, adding dryly, "Or at least more conventional?"

Annette laughed. "That was my last resort."

The woman looked like she was going to ask another question so Annette moved to look at the display shelves. The antiques were carefully arranged and polished but they were not grouped at all so Annette felt as if she were inside someone's house, a visitor who was both welcome and intrusive. There were china figurines next to delicate, leather-bound books; pictures in gilt frames next to a collection of dress rings laid in a black velvet case; a butterfly in a bell jar and a stuffed owl peering from a high shelf. The woman was watching her, so she said inanely, "Wow, you've got loads of stuff here. It only looks a tiny place from the front."

"Thank you. It is my hobby as well as my livelihood."

"That's lucky."

The woman placed another pair of candlesticks on the counter; these were china with a blue flowered pattern. Annette obediently examined them.

"How long have you had the shop?"

"How long? Twenty-five, no, twenty-six years this spring."

"Oh. That's – a long time." Annette surveyed the shelves again. "Do you mind being surrounded by this old stuff all the time? I mean, don't you feel like you're living in the past?"

The woman frowned. "What an odd question. No, of course not. The past is alive. All this – old stuff

– as you call it, is far more real than the plastic rubbish and chipboard you find these days."

Annette smiled tightly. "Oh – what's that? Are those emeralds?"

The woman turned; she looked for a moment too long before saying carefully, "The earrings? Oh, nothing much – some paste, rather old-fashioned. Now I do have some 1920s pieces you might like – I do find they translate very well to the current fashions."

Annette wasn't listening. She stepped round the carved umbrella stands at the end of the counter for a closer look but the shelf was too high for a clear view; and the green earrings were attached to a cloth of the same colour.

"May I see them?"

The woman reluctantly pushed a stool towards the shelf and climbed up to take the box, but as she stepped down, she stumbled and fell. The earrings fell to the floor and vanished under the counter, leaving the woman holding the empty box. Annette darted forwards to help her.

"Gosh, are you okay?" Annette helped the woman up and led her to a chair. "Sit down for a moment – did you hurt yourself? You look a bit shaken."

The woman forced a smile. "I'm fine. Really. Thank you."

Emeralds

She tried to get up but Annette said, "Maybe wait a bit, till you feel better ... Don't want you fainting on me!"

The woman was still holding the empty box. Annette saw there was a piece of paper inside; it must have been underneath the fabric holding the earrings in place. There was something written in Arabic script.

"Oh – the earrings were from Cairo," the woman said, seeing Annette's puzzled frown. "I think this must be the manufacturer's details, or something."

"My mother lived in Cairo," Annette said. "She was English but she worked there for a bit; she was a nanny to some children when she met my father. He's Egyptian. A trader. Import-export, that kind of stuff."

A trader. The feel of cool, perfect emeralds on soft, sun-warmed skin; reaching out over silk cushions embroidered with silver threads and songbirds; the touch of fingers twining together.

"How come you've ended up here?" the woman said softly, as if to herself.

Annette hesitated; she didn't usually talk about her background. But something – the warm circle of the shop, or the shock of the woman's fall – some echo of a place she didn't know – something made her answer. "My mother died when I was born and my father sent me back to live with my aunt and uncle in England. Of course they're my mum and dad really now. They adopted me, but my father in Egypt keeps in touch – birthday cards ..." Annette tailed off. She glanced again at the slip of paper from the jewellery box. A tiny thing, lodged there for all these years.

"Egypt is a beautiful country. I visited once or twice, on business," the woman said.

"Would you go back again?"

The woman shook her head, and stood up, wincing slightly and rubbing her elbow. "I have no reason to go back … The candlesticks – were any of them suitable?"

Annette ran her hand over the carving on the wooden set. "Yes, I'll take these, thank you. You know, officially my birth mother died from complications following childbirth. But my mum – aunt – said she died of sadness. My father lost someone once and he never got over it. He tried … We weren't enough."

The woman looked away and Annette caught the shine of tears. She opened her bag for her purse. A notebook inside fell open and a white page flickered.

"Mind if I borrow this pen for a moment?"

"Help yourself." The woman was busy with tissue paper and tape, not looking. Annette picked up the pen and began to write quickly. She tore off the sheet, tucked it in her pocket and replaced the pen.

"Thanks."

The woman placed the neat parcel on the counter. "I hope the lady at work likes them. It's a kind thought."

"Perhaps. But, if I'm honest, I'm doing it for Hippy Helen."

Emeralds

"Your old tutor?"

"Yes. I heard this morning. Cancer. She was fifty-one."

Scorched cotton and the scratch of sand; sweat and salt and the sting of her own voice. The clatter of a bracelet of emeralds flung onto polished tiles. Engine oil and the screech of metal as a train heaved its carriages out of the desert.

"I'm fifty-one," the woman said. "I should never have come back."

Annette fingered the slip of paper in her pocket, uncertain whether to say any more. She saw Hippy Helen, earnestly explaining some difficult point in one of her lectures. A shaft of sun from one of the high windows caught her hair and the white blonde became silver; she looked as if she belonged elsewhere; a traveller in an ancient caravan silently treading through the shifting paths of the Sahara.

"You're right," Annette said. "You shouldn't have come back. The box of emerald earrings – there was a message written. For you."

The woman shook her head, not understanding, but her eyes flashed for an instant. Green eyes.

Annette held out the slip of paper. "I translated. Arabic. It's what I studied at uni."

The woman took the paper, not speaking, not breathing. Annette glanced at the window; the pale light of winter was falling away into soft flakes of snow; people hurried by, shaking umbrellas open, trying to get home before the weather closed in.

"Oh! The earrings – they dropped on the floor as you fell, remember?"

The woman had not moved; she was still holding the unfolded paper. Annette glanced down. "Here's one." She bent down, and saw the other earring under the chair. As she reached for it, her bracelet, hidden by the sleeve of her jacket, slid down her wrist. Emeralds, linked by a delicate gold chain. The only gift he had ever given.

Annette placed the earrings on the counter. "Thank you for the candlesticks."

The woman did not seem to hear. Annette picked up the parcel and began to walk towards the door.

"Wait! The message – where, after all this time – I mean, how could I possibly find – it's been too long …"

Annette smiled. "It's okay. I wrote down the address as well." She opened the shop door and the swirling snow blurred the familiar outline of the High Street; glancing back she saw the woman carefully open the slip of paper and begin to read.

PANADA

Tanya D. Ravenswater

"Ricky? Are you awake, son? It's ten o'clock," Dulcima called up the stairs. Ricky twitched at the sound of his mother's voice. In the chinked light through the bedroom curtains, the waxy horn of his big toenail gleamed above the horizon of the bedstead. Otherwise, the room lay on, in its usual somnolent, dishevelled darkness, like the floor of some primordial forest, breathing ripe fungus and fermented fruit.

In Dulci's kitchen, the damp, scoured bottom of the milk-pan crackled and hissed on the electric element. In went the milk and a good knob of Dromena butter. None of your skimmed milk and half-fat nonsense for Dulci. The milk had to be just past blood-heat, which meant minding it carefully, testing it with your little finger. Everything else was done. Trimmed white bread dice in the pudding dishes. Tea brewing under the wadding of the hen cosy. Spoons polished on a pressed tea-towel printed with a worn-out Irish Blessing. Sugar bowl full to the brim.

"Des?" Dulci knew her husband's uneven step, his grunting effort in the hall as he pulled on his dusty moccasin slippers that she talcumed every night, while the dog was out doing his business and God only knew what else.

"Is Ricky awake yet, Des?"

"Right you be, Dulci. Panada's ready, is it?" Des heard what he wanted to hear.

"It'll just be a minute. You go through, Des. The telly's on."

Dulci took the pan to the dishes and tipped the warmed milk over the bread. She sighed, dredging each dish with sugar. It was hard to believe how much that bread could soak up. You thought you'd drowned it, but then there it was, asking for more, sponging up your last drop. Every blessed time Dulci made panada, she remembered being a girl on Torarm beach, running to and fro, dumping bucket after bucket of caster sugar sand into the water, believing that one day she would soak up the whole sea. But she never did.

"I'm takin' up Ricky's panada, Des," Dulci said, passing Des his dish. "I'll heat mine up later. Your cup's on the mantelpiece."

"You're awful good to us, y' know," Des replied, absent-mindedly, without taking his eyes off the News. Dulci always put the bowl right into your hands.

Ricky was almost sitting up in bed. The thought of rearranging his clumped pillows was too much. His hooded eyes began to close again.

"Let's be havin' you up that bed now, son. You'll choke on your panada lyin' down like that." Dulci cleared a space for the dish among the debris on

Ricky's bedside table. The layered litter of fudge wrappers and blackened banana skins accumulated as fast as she could clear it away.

"You'll give us a wee lift, won't y', Mum?"

His Mum was an awful fit woman for someone in their seventies. She was all muscle and no extra weight. His Mum was as strong as a racing greyhound. And whatever she said, there was nothing she liked more than looking after him and his Dad. Dulci plumped Ricky's pillows, then hooked her sinewed arm under his fleshy shoulder.

"Mind and watch ... m' *toe* ..."

"Right y' be, son. One ... two ... three ... hup!"

Keeping his prized right toenail in the air, Ricky pushed down on the bed with his left foot. The lift defied physics, but Dulci's courage always got them there in the end.

"Can you manage the panada yourself, Ricky? Or ... do y' want me to spoon it in t' you, son?" Dulci didn't need an answer. Growing that nail was taking everything out of him. It was taking everything out of Dulci as well. But sure, you'd do anything you could for your only begotten child. Panada was the best way of getting nourishment into him since the dentist had pulled all his big teeth. Not that Dulci had disagreed with Mr McNab. All those chews and fruit juice between meals had turned them rotten. It was just like when he was a wain again, pulling down on the spoon, as he had done on her breasts. All gums, no teeth.

Lost and Found

Des had taken early retirement from the buses because of his back problem. Ricky had never been employed. While the doctor had never been quite able to put a finger on what was wrong with him, he knew that Dulcima and Des were good people. There'd be no harm in keeping that family together. He was happy to sign Ricky off. *Fatigue and growing pains*, in an impressive but indecipherable hand, did the trick.

Ricky and Des had spent the years together tinkering with Ricky's old Ford Escort and completing five-thousand-piece sunset jigsaws. The car had been a present for Ricky's eighteenth birthday. Des had no trouble driving it back from the garage, but that was the only journey it had made in the twenty years since. He reckoned there had to be some problem or other and it was probably staring him in the face, but even with their combined brain power, he and Ricky couldn't figure it out. One day, Ricky kept saying, they'd be rolling in it. One day that car would get fixed and he'd drive into the town and get himself a decent job.

They had come up with the idea of growing Ricky's toenail while poring over the greasy pages of an out-of-date *Guinness Book of Records*. Ricky particularly admired an elderly Chinese man with a wispy floor-length beard, who cultivated a thumbnail so long he needed help with all aspects of daily living. In a moment of sheer genius, his Dad decided it might be an act worth following. Ricky had shown a talent for growing his big toenail. It could be the opportunity of a lifetime.

Dulci's own emery boards were too lightweight for Ricky's nail. Des supplied a gargantuan metal file. It had become a daily ritual after breakfast panada: Ricky's pedicure, then his bed bath. They couldn't risk that nail tearing at this stage.

"Don't be takin' too much off." It was the closest Ricky had ever come to feeling a surge of adrenaline. His future depended on that nail.

"Stop your panickin', will y'?" The nail business was starting to try even Dulci's patience.

"There wouldn't be just ... a tinchy bit more ... panada ...?" Ricky asked, feebly. "Feel ... shattered ... after m' bath, y' know ..."

Dulci's hand was on the door handle. Ricky was washed, dressed and in clean sheets, his right foot propped high, the nail looking its best. Dulci had been thinking about her panada in the kitchen, under a saucer. And a cup of sweet strong tea.

"Course there is, son. Just a minute and I'll fetch it up."

Ricky drifted contentedly back to sleep. Downstairs, Des nodded off in front of the telly. When Dulci lifted the saucer on her panada, she knew it wouldn't do for Ricky. She'd have to nip out to the corner shop for an extra pint of milk. They wouldn't even know she'd gone.

Lost and Found

It was two o'clock on Dulci's Little Ben on the mantelpiece. Des woke to the zigzagging sound of a siren in the distance, his empty panada dish still in his lap.

"Dulci? Is there another cup o' tea? And one of your buttered biscuits?"

No answer. She must have popped out the back with the washing. He'd give her a couple of minutes, then try again.

"*Dad?* I've been waitin' on her for ages." It was Ricky shouting down from the bedroom.

"Think she's puttin' out the clothes." It wasn't like Dulci to keep Ricky waiting.

Two hours later, Dulci still wasn't answering. Ricky was getting hoarse. Des felt vaguely unsettled. He was parched. Dulci always made the tea and lifted his plate. He didn't know what to do. Except wait. She had to see to the dog as well.

Earlier, in the shop, Dulci had had a terrible sharp pain in her chest. Jean phoned for the ambulance. The hospital doctor told Dulci she'd probably had a heart attack. She'd have to go to Cardiac Care, stay on bedrest and let them look after her. People receiving such news didn't generally appear so relieved.

"Want us to call someone for you, pet? Hubbie?" Dulci's special nurse plumped the pillows and tucked her in. Such a wee dote. She needed feeding up.

"It'll do some time later on. They'll be alright in the meantime. Now, do y' know how to make panada, dear?"

SCUT, OR, THE RABBIT'S TALE

Mike Wood

"Curiouser and curiouser!" thought Alice as she pursued the White Rabbit through Marks and Spencer.

He stopped at the salad counter, and without so much as a buy your leaves, began to nibble the produce, tearing at the cellophane wrapping with his sharp front teeth before sampling first one delight and then another. A supervisor came by, but the training manual had obviously failed to cover such an eventuality, so she hurried away, no doubt to consult a superior.

Alice was delighted at the incongruity of it all and, had she not been so well brought up, might have joined in with the orgy of sampling and destruction. As it was, she watched as the Rabbit moved on to the fresh strawberries. Curiously, apart from the now absent supervisor, nobody seemed to notice the White Rabbit. However, Alice herself was drawing more and more attention. Although she could remember nothing of choosing clothes or dressing herself, she looked down to find herself dressed in a diaphanous fantasy reminiscent of dragonfly wings. Other shoppers were casting discreet glances at her, until the boldest approached her and asked her where she had bought such a vision of delight.

Scut, or, the Rabbit's Tale

She wasn't sure how she'd got there, nor what was going on. She vaguely remembered drowsily lounging under a tree, trying to read *Watership Down*, but being bored because there were no pictures. She'd been sitting by her older sister who was thumbing through her Marks and Spencer's catalogue, which was full of intriguing pictures which distracted her. Could she have fallen asleep and be dreaming all this? She didn't think so – she could smell the freshness of the greenery the White Rabbit was still munching, and she had yet to answer the lady who'd asked her where she'd bought her gossamer creation – it didn't feel like a dream, but how could one tell? And how should she answer the woman's enquiry? She didn't know the answer anyway – she was aware, though, that she was increasingly the object of attention of those crowding around her. She could smell the various perfumes mingling from the women pressing close by.

But then another thought fluttered into her mind. The dress seemed so light and fragile that she suddenly wondered if it was transparent, or at least translucent – and was she wearing any underwear? She daren't look down for fear that she wasn't – what would she do? And did this mean that this was a dream? She'd had dreams like that before.

Suddenly it occurred to her that she should break away from the crowd and escape up the nearby escalator to the lingerie department. That way she would avoid the lady's questions and would be able to rectify any underwear discrepancy. Besides, she could see a sales supervisor coming her way, presumably to see what was causing such a disturbance in her usually well-ordered department. But as she pushed towards the escalator, the white fur of the Rabbit brushed warmly past her legs, and he jumped on to the moving stairs, thought better of the venture, and attempted a retreat, eventually mustering enough downward speed to counteract the upward mechanical motion. He arrived at Alice's feet, a panicky, puffing bundle of white. His eyes looked up imploringly into Alice's, and she thought she saw the shadow of her own confusion reflected in the dark pink depths.

Detecting an ally in her dilemma, she clutched his warm, trembling presence tightly and stepped hurriedly on to the escalator, still conscious of being the centre of a considerable degree of unwanted attention. As soon as she stepped on to firm ground, the Rabbit squirmed free and scampered off, his white scut disappearing between shoppers' legs. Alice was again aware that nobody seemed to notice him, and as she had no need to follow him, she pressed her way through the clamour towards the lingerie display. Snatching at the first items she could see through the blur of her trauma, she pushed towards the changing room. A bemused attendant thrust into her hand two numbered plastic discs which she didn't understand, and she found herself a small, curtained cubicle.

It was the first time she'd been alone since the start of this mystery, and suddenly it was more than she could bear. Tears welled up in her green eyes as she fought the sobs which were rising up from her girlish heart. She remembered from somewhere back in her mind that if you cried too much you could end up swimming in salt water with a menagerie of strange creatures, and she couldn't face that possibility. She had hoped to make a proper assessment of herself as she stood in front of the full-length mirror, but her tear-filled eyes could find no focus, nor could her mind, which was in turmoil. She heard somebody sobbing wrenchingly, but realised that it came from her own quivering lips. Her fear was compounded by the thought that the sound of her sobs must surely bring the changing-room attendant, and how could she explain herself? Anxious to escape this additional terror, she found herself stepping forward into the mirror.

Her sobs and sorrow seemed to be left behind in the cubicle, unable to make the transition through the glass. She didn't understand that, but there were so many things that had puzzled her today. She was glad at least to be feeling more cheerful.

She appeared to be in a field, but one chequered, like a chessboard. The square she was on was closely mown grass and had a faint sweet smell wafted on the breeze. Curious to discover more, she moved on to the next square which had soft, grey, fine foliage cropped close. She vaguely thought it might be camomile, with a sweet smell all of its own. It reminded her slightly of the smell of an anaesthetic she'd once had at the dentist, but in spite of the association it was pleasant and reviving.

"Reviving," she thought. "What do I need reviving from?"

She was no longer scampering on grass squares, but languidly rousing from a drugged sleep. Round her were hospital curtains, chequered in two shades of green, and she had a matching counterpane covering her body.

Just then her mother's head appeared through a gap in the curtains.

"Oh, thank goodness you've woken! We were really worried."

"But how did I get here?"

"Don't you remember? You fell down a steep bank. Your sister had to call the ambulance. They anaesthetised you. How are you feeling?"

She felt all right, she supposed, though a bit disoriented. But how could she explain to her mother why, under the counterpane, she was conscious of clutching Marks and Spencer's underwear, still in its wrappings, and two plastic numbered discs?

She noticed her mother had brought in her favourite old cuddly rabbit, tucked in by her pillow.

"Curiouser and curiouser!" the rabbit was thinking.

BUTCHER'S GRASS

Die Booth

He's mean. He has a mean sense of humour. He's arrogant and sexist and immature. He's talented, but I'm more talented; creative, but not like I'm creative. He's shorter than me and he's weedy, I could fit both of his chicken-wing legs into one of my rugby thighs. I have better hair. I have better style. I have better manners. He doesn't hold doors, or buy drinks, or listen. He can probably cook better than I can but that just puts him in the company of every other member of the human race.

I ask, "What do you see in him?"

"I don't *see* anything in him," and immediately it's there, that infuriating hint of a smile. It's the kind of smile you catch people doing when they daydream on buses, a sun-on-tarmac smile of secretive longing. "We're just friends."

Of course you are.

"Friends like you and me." It's not a question, it's an accusation. Now who's being childish? But I can't help myself: the guy just boils my piss. She laughs, two notes that sound more delighted than derisive.

"God no, nothing like me and you, you're a far better mate than he could ever be."

That's me: the best mate a girl could wish for.

It's difficult to get people to take you seriously as a man these days, when you have long hair and piercings. And a vagina. But one comfort is that I must be a real man if I can be physically the same as a woman and yet still understand them so little.

"What does she see in him?" I ask my friend Gareth.

Gareth sniffs and says, "Beats me. He's a wanker."

"Thanks for clarifying that."

"I don't know," Gareth says, "I don't know what birds are into. They always seem to go for the annoying pricks, innit." His mobile phone buzzes and he squints then smirks at the screen, flicking his thumb to scroll. His lips move slightly as he reads and then he places the phone face down on the cartoon-green baize of the table and picks his pool cue up.

The phone buzzes again and Gareth says with little evident remorse, "Sorry mate. It's her that works behind the bar at the Head. She won't leave me alone."

I say, "If everyone thinks he's such a wanker, then how does he constantly get ahead in life?"

Gareth raises one shoulder in a shrug, "Shit floats," and then he pots the pink.

I ask my friend, Jen, to get the female perspective.

"What does he have that I haven't got?" A rogue expression of *don't make me answer that* flits across her face and I frown impatiently, "apart from that."

"I don't know. Sometimes you just fall for people; you can't help it. If it makes you feel any better," she turns the high beam of her charm full on me, "if I was her I'd well rather go out with you than him."

Oh, you are such a liar. Her approval is confidently offered like counterfeit currency, brassy and obvious.

"Don't tell me you fancy him too?"

"Don't be stupid, of course I don't!" she says: denial so quick and bright it virtually rings. She backs it up with another smile, wide and close-lipped. She tucks a piece of hair behind her ear, and then re-tucks it even though it's not fallen free.

I like animals, I like art galleries, I write poetry. I go to the gym three times a week and make mortgage payments and drive a reasonable, mid-range car. I'm the man that every woman is said to want, but there's something missing and I'm starting to think it isn't just *that*. I'll tell you what: all the nice girls and even the nasty ones, it's no myth that what they really crave is a bastard.

Tonight I am packaged immaculately; my chest flat, my shoulders broad, my distressed grey leather sneakers (size nine, high-end high street) scuffed to optimum effect. Around my neck is a long leather thong with a silver arrow-head pendant on it, which is really in this season. I look just like the kind of guy who looks like me. I can't be what she wants. I can't even be what *I* want.

"Hey, handsome."

That's how she greets me, always, and stands on tiptoe to loop her arms around my neck. Always, I take her hand and kiss it and for a second I glimpse the patterns on her skin, all little interlocking lines and triangles like snow up close, like she's made of stars. When she pulls away she's shining. And there he is, behind her; the shadow cast across her light. When she notices him, she says, "Hi," and they exchange an awkward quick hug that's mostly shoulder and then he has to hug me too, while I'm wishing him biblical misfortune.

A whole tide of acquaintances can't dilute his presence. I'm keeping secret watch as he hogs her attention, one ear on my conversation, one ear on theirs, hearing collectively little over the thump of club speakers. Just snippets. Just laughter. I see the catch of spinning light on her canine tooth as she throws back her head and laughs at his jokes and I can feel my top lip curl back in a sneer but I can't stop it.

"Forget it!"

I shake my head a little and hold up my hand, shush, but Gareth says, "She'll find out what he's like soon enough."

"She already knows what he's like."

"Then it's her own fault, ain't it?"

I want to say, no. I want to say that he's tricking her like the shit he is, she's too smart to fall for this so he's obviously using some kind of evil mind trick to control her, like some sex-pest magician. I don't want it to be her fault. I want to save her. She wants to save him. Nobody wants to save me. I wish that I could think of an argument that doesn't sound petty and childish when really all I want to do is yell "I hate you" and punch his smirking, quipping face in.

What I actually do is this. We all reconvene outside the front door at chucking-out time, huddling over cigarettes and woozy with booze. People peel off in twos and threes and when she declines my offer to drop her off at her house from the taxi on the way back to my place, I just nod and shrivel inside.

"I'm going to go back with Rob. To talk."

"Right. Make sure you use a condom."

The look she gives me is almost worse than knowing where she's going.

Giving up on the taxi idea, I walk home even though it's miles and it's late and there's a sulking mist of autumn rain hanging around my head. If it actually got its act together, if the sky split open and spat down a real storm, then it might sink all these unwanted images in my head. But it doesn't, and my thoughts are noisy and belligerent with bottled beer. I bet she thinks *he's not that bad really*. She thinks *I can change him; all he needs is the love of a good woman. All it takes is the one. There's plenty more fish in the sea. Why settle for hamburger when you could have steak? The grass is always greener ...*

Lost and Found

The grass is always greener. It makes me think of that stuff they put in butchers' windows, that garish, primary-hued, spiky plastic turf that holds all the bloody cut-up bits of animal. It's greener, that grass, but it's not real. With real grass, when you dig just beneath the surface, all you find is dirt.

The day afterwards, she phones me and asks me to come and pick her up from the building where his flat is. I almost don't go, but then I do. She's sitting on the front steps with her toes curled under and her red dancing shoes neatly side-by-side beside her, a twisting sigh of grey rising from her cigarette.

"He wasn't what I expected," she says.

No. They never are. I don't ask her to clarify.

Of her own accord, she adds, "At least I know what you are, Jamie."

"And what's that?"

"My dandy prince."

Charming. Well-mannered. Reliable. Fictitious.

I gather her into my arms and rest my chin on top of her yellow curls, and I wish that I had the balls to treat her badly.

BLOOD FLIES UPWARDS

Elizabeth Brassington

Saturday was the worst day of the week – bloody butcher's day. I was not allowed to use that word, but Mr corpse-face Colman really deserved it. He seemed deader than the cows hanging up in his shop. They looked as though they'd once had life in them, but if Mr Colman had hung from the hooks, no one would have fancied him for their Sunday dinner.

If you went to the shop late on Saturday, his nasty-looking wife would come in for the takings. You could see they hated each other by the way they didn't speak, but just exchanged glares. Then she died and he was left with Bullock, a colossal man, and "Miss Er–" to help him out in the shop.

Going there was worse than going to elocution on Fridays and stammering over a poem I'd been learning all week: "Lean out of the window, Golden Hair."

"Emphasis on the 'lean'. You are begging her, remember."

I begged Mr Colman, too. "Please-may-I-have-a-nice-piece-of-beef-not-more-than-five-shillings-and-a-pound-of-sausages-please."

I learned that by heart as well – so I didn't leave out the five shillings. We had to go to Colman's shop because he'd got our meat coupons, and we were renting one of his houses and sometimes owed him money.

I hated my Saturday errand and on the way I would jump over the cracks in the pavement for luck. I was hot and sweaty when I arrived, but soon cooled down because it was always cold in the shop. On freezing days the door was wide open, and in summer even the flies didn't bother to go in. One look at Mr Colman's face and they were off to the sweet-shop next door to settle on the Turkish Delight.

I joined the queue, next to the line of dead animals. I was always surprised to see the blood dripping into the sawdust, because the carcasses looked so dry. They were like headless roundabout horses, with stiff, outstretched legs and necks. They should have had "Thumper" or "Galloper" written in fancy letters across them.

The queue took fairy-steps forward, but no one dared to speak. If you talked about the weather or clothing coupons, it was like laughing in church. Somebody once said "Nice day" to Mr Colman. He was so shocked, he had a fit of coughing all over the meat and the next person to be served changed their order to a tin of corned beef.

Sometimes when you were in the queue, there'd be a loud banging on the floor and everyone would jump back. Then a trap-door would open as Bullock came up through the floor like the Demon King in the pantomime – only not so fast. He'd be carrying a pig or a lamb over his shoulder, just like the Good

Shepherd in my book of Bible stories, but this time the wolf had got there first. Bullock would stare blankly round as the trap-door slammed shut and he lifted the poor animal on to a hook. The sawdust on the floor would spring up into the air, except where it was stuck by blood, then settle itself down again. The people in the queue always stared in silence until Bullock stumped off into the back room, where he could be seen hacking at chunks of meat with a blood-stained cleaver. I sometimes thought that Miss Er–, who took the money, may have given him a little smile occasionally, but it was probably just my imagination.

When the meat was slapped on to the scales, Mr Colman would shout out the price: "Five-and-sixpence, Miss Er–".

I hated paying because I was sorry for Miss Er–: she looked so cold and sad. Everyone said she was a poor relation, who relied on Mr Colman for money and was forced to work in his freezing shop all day. She wore damp mittens and had a dew-drop on her nose which sometimes fell into the till. Her fingers were shaky when she counted out the change, and she always whispered "Thank you" when you paid her, and gave a little smile. Afterwards we'd both look at Mr Colman to see if he'd noticed.

One day, Mum decided to try a nice piece of pork for a change, as well as the sausages, and I got into a state, trying to learn the new order. I was so busy doing this that I forgot to watch the cracks in the pavement and fell over. When I got out a hanky to tie round my knee, a sixpence slid out of my glove and fell down a drain. What if I couldn't now afford all the sausages and Mr Colman had to take some back off the scales? You can't join up a link of sausages once it's been cut.

I ran all the way, but it was late when I got to the shop and all the customers had gone. I was amazed to see that Mr Colman wasn't behind the counter as usual, and that Bullock and Miss Er– were in charge. I was puffed out, but so relieved that it was only Bullock serving me that I got the order right first time. I'd picked up my soggy parcel when I heard the usual banging on the floor. We all turned to stare, and Bullock made his way round the counter towards the trap-door. He yanked it up by the handle and Mr Colman's head and shoulders came into sight. He was holding a big bundle of papers covered with rows of numbers.

Bullock's fingers must have been slippery with blood, because somehow he seemed to lose his grip on the handle. There was a horrible crunching sound and a spray of blood shot into the air as the trap-door slammed down. Mr Colman disappeared swiftly and silently from sight.

I grabbed the meat so hard that my fingers went right through the newspaper and into the squishy sausages. I think that Bullock and Miss Er– had forgotten I was there. As I ran out of the shop, I couldn't help looking back. They were just standing there, staring at each other.

When I got home, Mum asked me if I'd managed to get the pork. I just nodded.

Three weeks later, when the shop was open again, Bullock and Miss Er– were behind the counter. When Bullock had weighed out my meat, he looked at Miss Er– and said, "Five-and-tenpence, please, Lavinia." He stared at me for a moment, then cut off an extra sausage and put it in my parcel.

As I left the shop I noticed a strip of artificial parsley, neatly arranged round the trays of lights and liver. Miss Er– leaned over into the window with a dish-cloth in her hand and smiled at me as she wiped a blob of bloody liver from a clump of bilious green leaves.

A SEARCH FOR SIMEON

George Horsman

"This must be where they camped."

Alice pointed across the field. Empty grassland stretched 200 metres to a towering parapet of lime trees that stirred drowsily in the morning breeze. At the end, three blocks of semi-detached houses impinged on what must previously have been part of the field but which was now fenced off into small gardens.

"Are you sure?" Geoff's tone was sceptical. "It was forty years ago and all we have to go on is the mark you say your father pencilled on an old map."

"There's his diary, too. It says, 'past the Bull and Bush'. That won't have moved."

"There are so many fields."

"Not with lime trees at the end. And they're old – look at their size."

They hadn't meant their visit to turn out like this. Taking a week's break at a guest house in Kington twenty miles away, they'd merely heard that Thornton was a picturesque village and had driven over to see it. Only when they'd left the car and wandered into the village square, leafy with plane trees and sycamores draped in the satin of late autumn sunshine, had Alice stopped short.

"Heavens! I've just remembered. This is where they came for their honeymoon – my parents, during the war. They camped in a field here. I remember it from the diary my father kept."

"Camped?"

"They'd no money. He'd done six weeks in Wandsworth Jail for refusing to join up – a conscientious objector – and then he'd been sent to work on a farm up north. While he was there he proposed to Mum by post – they'd met in Germany before the war and then both become language teachers. So this was his first holiday from the farm and also his honeymoon. On another farm."

"Past the Bull and Bush, you say. Let's go and see."

And so the search had begun. They found the stream her father's diary mentioned and stood above a faint declivity in the grassland which might have been the remains of the crater made when, in the minutely written words of Simeon's diary, "a German bomber, either lost or driven back by our ack-ack over Birmingham, jettisoned its last bomb". The more they explored, the surer Alice became that they'd found the right place.

The narrative of that tense, introverted man ran like a silent film in her mind. Why had he refused to fight? Not from sympathy with Hitler's Germany – though after living there for two years he'd never once, in her recollection, spoken against the regime.

He simply said, "I lived and worked with them. They're my friends. I can't go and kill them."

Yet there were others he'd damaged. Joan, for one. The wife he should have loved most.

Joan had always come second to his love of study. Born to a railwayman father in a household always penurious, and himself niggardly in spending, he'd given his soul to education as to a rope that would pull him out of poverty and deprivation. But the rope had itself ensnared, entangling his hands and feet, even in the end his mind.

Alice remembered the countless evenings he'd devoted to studying for degrees, first in French, then in Spanish and later Russian; the enforced silence in the house; the smoke from his unbroken chain of cigarettes. And with the ever-mounting toll of educational qualifications had come a spreading, cold detachment from the world and from his family. Alice tried to recall any conversation in the house which hadn't ended in bickering or a quarrel. She tried to remember a single happy outing or domestic evening the family had enjoyed together; a single time when Simeon wasn't taciturn, cut off like an ascetic monk from warmth and happiness. But none came.

Abstraction weakened the power to assess his own abilities. There'd been one stage in the 1960s while she was in the sixth form when he'd been convinced that Britain and America were doing something wrong in foreign affairs and *knew* he could have done better. She remembered the break in his high-pitched voice, which she later came to associate for some reason with the cerebral palsy that killed him in his fifties – a year after Joan, too, died. "If only they'd ask me. I could do it. They don't *know* Russia. They don't *understand* the people."

The intensity of his conviction amounted almost to frenzy. Yet he himself had never visited Russia, let alone known the Kremlin and its ruler. His knowledge came only from books, and those the literary works of past centuries.

Education, she thought. Does it really educate?

"Were you grief-stricken when he died? You must have felt loss."

Alice shrugged, as if shaking off troubled thoughts. "I never knew him."

And in truth there'd been little grief. Sometimes in Alice's early days, sunk in thought, he'd performed his duty of walking her to school, and once, longing to love and worship this tall lean man who was her daddy, Alice had held her hand up to take his. At first he hadn't noticed; but when, in the end, he'd grasped the tiny upstretched fingers he'd done so with such indifference that the whole surge of her devotion dissolved to bitterness. If he'd only smiled, only once given her hand a tiny, answering squeeze she would have been his – Daddy's Girl. But he never did.

"Let's go to the tea-shop. It looked cosy – all oak beams and inglenooks."

"Good idea. They might have gone there, too."

"He did spend, sometimes?"

"Now and then. But seldom."

Childhood penury had frozen parsimony into him. Simeon. The very name was severe, distant. Sometimes, Alice remembered, her mother had called him Sim. But always, when it happened, there'd been faint embarrassment, a feeling that the name conjured up a happy intimacy that no longer had the ring of truth, that had died long ago. By the time Alice reached the sixth form there were no family outings or games. Shared holidays lay in a forgotten past.

They sipped their tea in silence. It was when Geoff went to the cashdesk to pay that Alice – as if her husband's brief absence somehow removed Simeon from her life all those years ago – felt memories flit like moths into the dim-lit cavern of her mind.

One was a mere phrase, a mindless jingle: *Plush, the man with the velvet waistcoat.* There'd been a time when Simeon had often said that; it was one of his catchphrases. He'd said it when he rocked her on his knee in the early days, when she was still a toddler. An absurd, meaningless phrase, yet jocular, like an uncle's inevitable joke.

And the other time, an afternoon walk. It, too, had been in autumn. Alice could remember the beech leaves curling out like ginger-snap from dry twigs, their bevelled edges crinkled with soft rust. For once Simeon had been jolly. No, not jolly. The word suggested a rubicund, jovial man and Simeon had never been that. But humorous, witty in his shrewd way, his eyes bright with the glee of making her and her mother laugh. *Plush, the man with the velvet waistcoat.* Had he said it that afternoon? Alice couldn't recall. But the memory – or its counterfeit – persisted. It was the sort of thing that, in softer mood, he might have said.

Among the trees of Briscote Wood they'd played hide and seek – a game she usually played just with her mother, her favourite game when she was six. Simeon had hidden especially well and then, just when they were about to give up looking, had sprung out: *Whoosh!* Perhaps it was then that he'd chanted the jingle about Plush. How she'd laughed! The afternoon had sped by. Alice hadn't been able to believe it was tea-time, with her not a bit hungry, when her mother had joshed them to the last bus home.

And there, on the top deck, Joan had cried.

"What's the matter, Mummy?" Alice was puzzled and upset.

"Nothing, love. I just… Don't worry."

"But what's the matter?"

"Nothing." Joan dried her eyes. But a few minutes later, when Alice looked back at her, her cheeks were wet again, with the tears of knowing, on that one afternoon, happiness in the family. The tears of knowing it would never return.

They left the café and went out into the autumn air. A sycamore had turned yellow in the old village square; but one or two of its leaves, as if in deliberate contrast, burned in brilliant red.

Lost and Found

Red, Alice thought with glistening eyes: the colour of plush. The man with the velvet waistcoat.

TIGHTEN THE CORD AROUND HIS NECK

Andrew Bogle

They will call him the bog man, after the place where he was found, by men harvesting the ancient peat. They will cradle and lift this exciting find, wordless almost in his presence. They will transport him to a laboratory where the lights shine brighter than any solstice sun; their bleached lab coats are whiter than any grains of sand and the howling of midnight wolves has never been heard.

They will marvel at the hair surviving on his head, at his once-skin turned to leather. They will prise away the enclosing peat remnants to reveal more of his twisted form. All the while, preserving water will sprinkle over him like the endless mists through which he walked. They will measure his height and weight in units alien to him, carbon dating him to the Iron Age. They will be meticulous in their studies, noting his manicured nails; that his beard and moustache were trimmed by shears; a man of some importance, evidently. His last meal was unleavened bread prepared upon a heather fire, they will conclude.

And his death? That's the biggest puzzle of all. The scholars and archaeologists will speculate, try and tease out some sense or meaning from his brutal end. No tests, though, can replicate the seeing of his dead eyes or the listening of his closed ears. There has not been invented any scientific measure of love or fear. They cannot know him.

They cannot know that his small band travelled far on horseback over uncertain trails, their ailing guide coughing and spitting all the way. They are riding into the jaws of their enemy. Blood of the two warring tribes has run red from grandfather to father and from father to son. Enough. His father believes that their mission will restore peace. Pray to the gods that his father is right. He looks around, seeing the fear in his companions' downcast faces. He swallows hard, his own throat dry.

They reach their destination at sunset on the third day. The shadow of the huge earth mound hangs over them. The camp is protected by circles of ditches and pointed wooden stakes driven into the ground. He has never seen anything made by man so grand or foreboding. The guards eye them suspiciously and talk in a strange rasping tongue. They must put down their weapons, the guide translates. His horse shifts uneasily, reluctant to move forwards. One of his group says that animals can smell treachery. He calms the horse then nods his assent. His sword is snatched from his grasp.

Inside the compound, barefoot children ogle at the strangers. Hens and piglets scuttle out of their way. They are led to the great wooden hall and, in the darkness of the packed building, he can dimly make out a fearsome grey-haired figure seated on a throne. He walks slowly forwards with eyes averted, and then kneels, holding out upturned palms to signal his obedience. The chieftain rises, stands over his defenceless form. One blow could kill him. Instead, the other man grasps both hands, lifts him up and embraces him. He presents the chieftain with a tribute, a silver bracelet intricately worked, that glistens despite the gloom. A murmured approval echoes around the hall.

They feast with their hosts that night, tearing at fistfuls of wild boar, ramming bread into their hungry mouths. He washes the food down with a potent brew that burns his throat and makes the room sway. The chieftain talks earnestly, the guide translating. To cement their new-found alliance, the chieftain's daughter will become the woman of his brother. He says that the chieftain does his father and all of their tribe a great honour and that his brother is the most fortunate of men.

Their faces grow warmer by the light of the fire. More logs are added, together with some sprigs of heather which crackle, releasing a rich perfume. He has heard that the chieftain's daughter is very beautiful. You must see her, the chieftain responds. He stands to greet her. They bow at a distance. She sits down beside her father who hands the bracelet to her. She turns it over and over in her palms, an object of wonder. She looks across and thanks him for the beautiful gift. That's when he's lost: when she looks at him. He offers some pretty inconsequence about no beauty matching her own and she smiles, before lowering her gaze and tracing with her fingertips the graceful silver swirls.

The chieftain is in full swing now. They will make common cause against a third tribe, an irritant to them both. The chieftain will take the copper mine and the rich grazing lands to the west, they can have the remainder of the territory and both will sell off as slaves any survivors of the unwanted tribe not butchered in battle. He nods agreement to the master plan but his thoughts return constantly to the daughter. Sidelong he watches as she holds her hands out to the fire and slowly turns her wrists better to marvel at the dazzling silver and its yellow flame reflections. She turns, imperceptibly, so her father will not know, and looks at him unblinking, that shared look confirming the bond between them. Later, when she leaves, both stand at a distance and bow before she walks slowly past him and, unseen, strokes her fingers against his hand.

In a fevered sleep, images of her, from the intricate braiding of her hair to that elusive smile, echo in his skull. Now she calls to him, beckoning him closer. Reaching out to touch her, he wakes and the potent vision fades, diluted by the thin dawn light. They must leave. He lingers, hoping in vain for another sight of her. He will have to wait until the planned-for nuptials. Their ailing guide is too ill to travel so the chieftain furnishes a replacement. They begin their weary way back. There are arrangements to be made for the union of his brother and the chieftain's daughter. He doubts he can stomach it. Let dynasties fall, let his father and brother be run through with his own treacherous sword, let the chieftain vow to wreak terrible destruction; if he is ever to know peace, he must have her for his own.

They are riding next to a steep wooded escarpment he does not recognise. The new guide reassures him with an easy smile. This is a shortcut that will save them half a day. That evening under the eternal starscape they eat some more of the bread given to them while screeching owls call overhead.

He is awoken before dawn by a sword-point at his throat. In the half-light he can make out his companions, lifeless on the ground. The guide grins with his captors. They drag him along with a rope round his neck. If he stumbles they do not slow down. They beat him when the fancy takes them. He tells the guide of his importance, how he could be ransomed for more gold and silver than they can imagine. The guide advises him not to waste his breath. He has betrayed him to the third tribe. They do not deal in such niceties, only death.

The acidity of the bog is what preserves him so well. He will be freeze-dried and put on display. Shuffling crowds will read the printed notes beside the exhibit, recording his fate, how he suffered two axe blows to the back of his head and was pummelled so violently in the back that his ribs were broken, before the thin cord still visible around his neck squeezed the last drop of life out of him. The rest will be forever beyond our knowing.

We cannot know that he is forced to kneel on the sodden ground. He waits for death. They intone words beyond his understanding. He cannot know that all of us are like insects caught in amber, each enmeshed in our own time. He can guess perhaps that the best of us is what we leave behind. He waits. He tries to pray to the gods of the land, the air and the water but all he can think of is the girl with the fire playing in her eyes. He waits. The last things he sees are the stagnant water and the rushes bending in the wind.

THE KILLER SENTENCE

Miriam Sulhunt

"Tonight, we shall discuss the importance of the first sentence." Millicent Morrow's beady eyes darted around the room. She patted her crest of silver hair, but before she could continue a pale, willowy girl raised her hand.

"Er, we have a new member."

Millicent nodded in my direction.

"I'm Jane." I gushed. "I can't tell you how thrillled ..."

"Yes, of course you are." Millicent interrupted impatiently.

Rebuffed, I flipped open my notebook and assumed an air of nonchalance as she went on.

"The first sentence is crucial ..."

The pale, willowy girl cleared her throat noisily.

"What is it now, Hermione?"

"Barbara isn't here yet."

Millicent tapped her watch. "I can't hang around all evening waiting for latecomers," she said tetchily.

Hermione pulled a face. A blonde girl with dangly earrings stifled a giggle. Millicent frowned.

"Your opening salvo," she said, enunciating the words with a certain weariness, "must grip the reader by the throat ..."

A commotion in the doorway caused her to break off with an impatient "Tsk" as a ruddy-cheeked woman with one leg heavily bandaged limped into the room.

"What happened to you?" Hermione's voice was brimming with concern.

"Monty threw me and I landed in a ditch." The woman guffawed loudly.

"Can we get on, Barbara?" said Millicent. "It's ten past seven already." She drummed her fingers on the table before going on. "Your first sentence must hook the reader before he even ..." The rest of Millicent's words were drowned out by a scraping sound as Barbara dragged two chairs out from the table, sank onto one of them and extended the bandaged leg across the other.

"I have to keep it elevated," she explained.

"That's right. You could get a blood clot," said a plump girl with mousy hair. "My cousin got a clot and she nearly died."

Millicent gave an exasperated sigh. "Can we talk about our ailments after the meeting?" She took a deep breath. "The first sentence must shock, surprise or mystify, in as few words as possible. It must hit your reader right between the eyes. *Bam!*" She thumped the table and we all jumped. "Let's hear what you have come up with. Who would like to start?"

A freckle-faced girl next to me raised her hand.

"Fire away, Sue," said Millicent.

The Killer Sentence

Opening a thick folder, Sue began. "A crescent moon hung over the car park and myriads of stars twinkled merrily in the firmament."

A long silence followed.

"Dull," said Millicent finally.

Sue sagged in her chair.

"I quite liked it," said Hermione soothingly.

"You've got to start somewhere," added Barbara.

Millicent pursed her lips. "Your book, I take it, is a slow burner. Not something I would recommend for a first novel." She looked around the room. "How can Sue inject some *va va voom* into her lacklustre first sentence?"

We were gaping blankly at one another when the door was flung open. A man carrying a large sheaf of papers came in. He was about forty, balding, with ginger stubble. Not a good look.

"Ned Carter," he said, flopping onto a chair.

Hermione mouthed the words "Welcome Ned," but Millicent simply ignored him.

"Remember, Sue, the opening sentence of your novel must grip the reader from the get-go. Perhaps we can draw inspiration from some of the most memorable first lines ever written. 'It was the best of times, it was the worst of times.' 'The past is a foreign country: they do things differently there.' Need I go on?"

"'I was born in the year 1632 in the city of York'," said Ned.

"Eh?" said Millicent.

"The opening sentence of *Robinson Crusoe*." Ned leaned back lazily in his chair. "Some might say it's bland, even banal. Yet, in my opinion, it is the beginning of one of the greatest novels ever written."

Millicent placed the tips of her fingers together as she replied with a studied casualness. "Have you published anything, Fred?"

"Ned."

"What?"

"It's Ned. Actually I was long listed for the Charmian Sprott Fiction prize in 2010 and in 2011 my play for hospital radio, *Bloodbath on Ward Ten*, was highly commended."

Hermione leaned towards him. "Well done," she said, her voice all breathy.

Millicent sniffed loudly. "Well, Ted," she began, "I have had a string of crime novels published. Maybe you have read them. My private detective solves crimes that have baffled Scotland Yard, using his psychic powers."

"Psychotic powers?" the mousy girl puzzled.

"Psychic powers. PSYCHIC," said Millicent testily. "The point I am attempting to make," she continued, speaking slowly and distinctly, "is that I know what I am talking about. At this early stage in your career you are writing not for your own pleasure, but for a commissioning editor. Unless your first sentence makes her eyes pop out of her head, your precious manuscript will end up on some slush pile."

"I don't agree." Ned stroked his nose with a bony forefinger. "I write for myself. For the journey. I like to set off slowly, sauntering, so to speak. I hope my reader will come along for the ride – it'll get bumpy as we go along, stopovers in fleapit motels, mean streets, maybe a mugging," Ned's eyes glinted, "but if they hang in there, keep up, stay the course, I guarantee my reader won't regret coming along for the helluva roller coaster ride of his life." He paused, smiling toothily.

"Fascinating," sneered Millicent. "Now, where was I? Ah! ... Your first sentence must introduce a dilemma ..."

Ned was not giving up. "I'd like to illustrate my point by reading aloud a chapter from my work in progress, *Infiltrating the Plasma Vortex*."

Millicent did not miss a beat. "Save your deathless prose for the long, winter evenings," she said.

I think we all breathed a sigh of relief. I certainly did. Ned, nettled, half rose from his seat. "This isn't working," he hissed.

"As I was saying," trilled Millicent, "you must begin at a crisis point in your central character's life ..."

"I'm leaving," announced Ned.

"Okey dokey," said Millicent. "Good-bye." Her eyes flickered over him briefly before she continued. "Your first words must draw the reader into your world. My own bestselling novels ..."

Hermione clutched at Ned's sleeve. "Don't go yet," she whispered urgently.

"My own bestselling novels ..." repeated Millicent, raising her voice an octave as Ned slumped back into his seat, "available from Amazon, succeed in whetting the reader's appetite. He or she is compelled to race onwards to the next sentence and the one after that as I ratchet up the tension. My reader is well and truly hooked." She came to a triumphant halt.

I gazed at her with rapt admiration. My mind was made up. I would scrap the historical novel I had been working on and become a crime writer like Millicent. Perhaps I would win some award. What was it called? The Golden Blade? My bestselling books would make millions. I'd be able to chuck my dreary job ... A nudge from Sue jerked me out of my reverie.

"Millicent wonders if you have a first sentence you'd like to share." She nodded her head towards my notebook. Gazing in horror at what I now saw as pathetic ramblings, I was opening and closing my mouth like the guppy in my fish tank at home, when the door opened. A girl with spiky hair put her head round. She was jangling of bunch of keys.

"I've got to close the library early," she said, "Staff shortages. Soreeee."

Saved by the bell.

"Pity," said Millicent, gathering up her things. "We'll have to call it a day. I'll look forward to hearing your scintillating first sentences next time."

The Killer Sentence

We were silent as she pattered out of the door and along the corridor. Then Sue spoke.

"Millicent has left the building," she said.

"Good old Millicent." Barbara heaved herself upright and scratched at her bandage. "You know," she added, "I really did like your first sentence."

"Me too," I mumbled, as we drifted towards the door. Out of the corner of my eye I could see Hermione in a huddle with Ned.

"We're going for a drink at the Grapes of Wrath. Anyone fancy coming along?" she asked.

There was a murmur of assent as we trailed along the corridor and out through the library, passing through the crime section. As the door clanged shut behind us, I looked up at the sky. A crescent moon hung over the car park and myriads of stars twinkled merrily in the firmament.